Clement Was Oblivious To Everything

except the woman he was holding pressed against him with the flat side of his ax. He drew in her scent. Faintly sweet, faintly spicy, it smelled ... warm. The scientist in him shuddered at the crossing of sensory data, while another part, a part he scarcely recognized, stirred.

Reaching out, he recognized the delicate shape of humerus, clavicle and scapula and closed his fingers firmly over her shoulder. She was rigid.

"Exhale," he ordered, and she did, in a long, shuddering gust. Personal space forgotten, he leaned closer as, without his glasses, he attempted to examine her face.

Only gradually did he become aware of the soft mewing sound issuing from her throat. He wasn't hurting her. Hands that could hold a butterfly safely would never hurt a woman. But he was becoming increasingly aware of her *femaleness*. A certain softness in the mammary region ... the distinctive conformation of the pelvic girdle ...

Suddenly Clem stiffened. To his dismay, his mind wasn't the only part of him that noticed the differences. His body was starting to react with rather amazing enthusiasm!

Dear Reader:

As you can see, Silhouette Desire has a bold new cover design that we're all excited about. But while the overall look is new, two things remain the same. First, we've kept our eye-catching red border. You can be sure to always spot Silhouette Desires on the shelves! Second, between these new covers are the high-quality love stories that you've come to expect.

In addition, the MAN OF THE MONTH program continues with Mr. September, who comes from the pen of Dixie Browning. Clement Cornelius Barto is a unique hero who is sure to charm you with his unusual ways. But make no mistake, it's not just *Beginner's Luck* that makes him such a winner.

October brings you a man who's double the fun, because not only is Jody Branigan an exciting hero, he's also one of Leslie Davis Guccione's Branigan brothers. Look for his story in *Branigan's Touch*.

We at Silhouette have been happy to hear how much you've all enjoyed the Year of the Man. The responses we've received about the special covers— and to each and every one of our heroes—has been enthusiastic. Remember, there are more men ahead in 1989—don't let any of them get away!

Yours,

Lucia Macro
Senior Editor

DIXIE BROWNING

BEGINNER'S LUCK

SILHOUETTE *Desire*

Published by Silhouette Books New York

America's Publisher of Contemporary Romance

SILHOUETTE BOOKS
300 East 42nd St., New York, N.Y. 10017

ISBN: 0-373-05517-X

First Silhouette Books printing September 1989

All the characters in this book are fictitious. Any
resemblance to actual persons, living or dead, is
purely coincidental.

®: Trademark used under license and
registered in the United States Patent and
Trademark Office and in other countries.

Printed in the U.S.A.

DIXIE BROWNING

writes about her contribution to Silhouette Desire's *Man of the Month* program: "When I was first invited to take part in this project, I thought, why not? If any woman ever had a head full of heroes, I do. It's about time one of them got more than second lead.

"But why did I have to choose Clem? Granted, the man was a challenge. If I didn't give him his chance, odds are that no one ever would, but the poor darling is practically inarticulate! Did you ever try to make conversation with a man who hasn't a clue how to go about it? And as for romancing a woman—!

"Well, I'll just leave you to be the judge. I still haven't recovered."

One

Clement was half asleep when the answering machine clicked on, and a disembodied voice filled the room. "Hattie? It's me—Martha. I'm on my way, but so much has happened that I might be a day or so earlier than we'd planned, if it's all right. Something's come up—there's this man, and—oh, I can't go into it now, it's too wild. But if I get in a real bind, I might call for you to come get me, and you're to let me know if it's inconvenient, because I can always—uh-oh, I'd better run. The others are waiting, and there he is again."

Lying on his back, nude except for his glasses—he always put on his glasses when the phone rang—Clement considered the words he'd just listened to. And then he considered the voice. It wasn't the first call the machine had taken from one of his great-aunt's flaky artist friends, but this one was...different somehow. Something in the voice intrigued him. Breathless was not quite the word to de-

scribe it, although there was an element of breathlessness—
as if the caller had been running. The voice was young,
southern and definitely female, but there was something
else. And it was that something else that bothered him.

It was some time later that it hit him. The something else.
She'd been nervous. In fact, she'd sounded almost...frightened.

Clement wasn't the sort to resent having his sleep dis-
turbed by a late-night call. In the first place, it was proof
that the phone he'd dropped, broken and repaired was still
working. In the second place, he'd always had an inquiring
mind, and in the third place, he was rather desperately
hoping to hear from his Great-aunt Hattie. She had dragged
him away from his work and up to her lair more than a
month ago to stay there and keep her pipes from freezing
while she cruised the Greek Islands with a bunch of her
wacky friends.

All in all, it was a fitting end to a lousy year. Two of his
best assistants had quit, supplies he'd requisitioned six
months ago had yet to show up and to top it off, Charles
Danforth had left, casting Clem in the role of acting administrator.

Protesting hadn't done a bit of good. He was about as
effective at registering protests as he was at dealing with
bureaucracy. Hell, he couldn't even communicate outside
the laboratory, everyone knew that. But as senior member
of B.F.I.'s Research and Development Department, he'd
been nailed when Danforth had left on short notice to go
with Lavorly Laboratories. They'd needed someone in a
hurry, and Clem's reflexes had been slow, thanks to a cold
that had come and gone all summer and then had finally
turned into pneumonia. He'd agreed to fill in during an
emergency that showed no signs of ending.

Even with his assistant doing most of the work, the stress had been intense. He'd succumbed to another round of mycoplasma early in October. Coughing his head off, he'd dragged around the lab, dragged around the office, doing a lousy job of everything. And since he hadn't taken a day of vacation in the six years he'd been there, no one could complain when he'd left.

Administrator! He wasn't sure if the job required an imbecile or a genius—all he knew was that it wasn't for him. If B.F.I. didn't find someone else to take over he'd hire out as a street sweeper! That, at least, wouldn't require him to file an endless stream of meaningless reports, which no one bothered to read. Or to attend endless meetings, listen to reams of drivel, while the real work he'd been hired to do grew stale.

Clem was not a social animal. Due to a combination of factors, he had never developed an easy way with people, and forcing it only made matters worse. Hattie Davenport was the only woman outside the laboratory—or inside, either, for that matter—with whom he could carry on anything resembling a normal conversation. They'd been friends since he was six years old, and being rather peculiar herself, she'd never considered him in the least bit strange.

Clem had missed her after she'd retired from teaching art and moved away to live in this Victorian hideaway in the Blue Ridge Mountains, where the nearest neighbor was four miles away over a rugged cross-country path. But he'd understood her need for solitude and self-sufficiency. At seventy-nine, Hattie was far more capable of looking after herself than he was at thirty-two, a fact of which both of them were aware.

He was pretty sure she'd had an ulterior motive for insisting that he house-sit for her while she went on her annual "one last fling." The pipes were in little real danger this early in the season, and her houseplants could be replaced. And few burglers ever made it this deep into the wilds of Buncombe County.

No, he knew Hattie pretty well after all these years. She'd decided it was time to Do Something About Clement again. Stranding him here with no way out had been her effort to force him to become more independent and self-reliant, and he'd been just miserable enough at the time to agree with her scheme. Up to a point.

But the point had long since been passed. He'd run out of things to read at the end of the first week. After going through the stack of technical material he'd brought with him, he'd been bored into exploring the countryside. It was a new experience—dealing with nature in the raw. To his surprise, he discovered he'd been missing an exhilarating adventure by spending his whole life indoors.

Within a week he was hiking miles each day, most of them vertical. He discovered wood chopping. There were fireplaces in most of the rooms, and Hattie's groundhog kiln devoured wood by the cord. He'd exercised, eaten and slept more than he had in years, and in his spare time he'd read through all the old newspapers and started in on Hattie's meager library, which consisted of art books, cook books and nineteenth-century erotica.

That had been a mistake. He was restless enough as it was.

Physically, Clem was completely recovered from his pneumonia. In fact, he'd never felt so fit in his entire life. He even looked different. The short brush cut that he'd found most practical and the neat beard he'd worn for the past half dozen years had grown all out of recognition. He was shaggy, his clothes no longer seemed to fit and he'd developed an astonishing supply of muscles and calluses!

If that added up to self-sufficiency, then Hattie had done her job well. But a man could walk only so many miles, chop only so many cords of wood, sleep only so many hours a day. The restlessness, that deep-seated, nameless emptiness that had been a part of him for as long as he could remember, was getting worse without his work to keep it at bay.

Clem checked the answering machine after coming in from a long hike, hoping for a call from his secretary saying that they'd found someone to take Danforth's place. He needed to continue his work on research. Four projects were sidelined until he could get back to them, and one of them had begun to look promising. But for reasons that were beyond him, the management at B.F.I. was being extremely negligent. It was as if they no longer cared whether new products were in the works or even if those being tested were given approval.

He'd tried calling, but even the switchboard was fouled up. His secretary, Ed Malvern, had been out every time he'd managed to get through, and finally he'd given up in frustration.

The second call came just before dark. It was the same voice. Soft, hesitant, it stirred an unfamiliar feeling inside him that had nothing to do with the words spoken.

Odd, he thought. Judging from the constriction of the larynx, she was either extremely self-conscious or extremely frightened. "Hattie, it's me—Martha. Be looking for me. I'm going to watch for a chance and slip away from the tour. If I can hitch a ride I will, and I may not have time to— Oh-oh, someone's coming! I'll tell you all about it when I see you."

Clem analyzed the message, more intrigued than he cared to admit even to himself over a few words spoken by a stranger. And a woman, at that. She was planning to visit his great-aunt. Evidently, she was expected, but certainly not so soon. Hattie was no stickler for detail, but not even she would invite a guest and then leave home.

Whoever the woman was, Clem devoutly hoped she would find it impossible to slip away—*slip away?*

What an odd way of putting it. Well, intriguing voice or not, Clem didn't wish her luck. If there was one thing he could do without, it was people, and especially people of the female variety.

It wasn't that he was a misogynist. The plain truth was that for all his accomplishments—seven degrees by the time he'd reached twenty-three, including bachelor's degrees in computer science, biology, mathematics and linguistics, master's degrees in chemistry and philosophy and a doctorate in chemical engineering, followed by two years at the prestigious Hastings Institute and an enviable position at Beauchamp Forbes International—the plain truth was that women intimidated him. They scared the hell out of him. When it came to social intercourse, he was a dropout.

The progeny of two brilliant minds, Clem often suspected his parents had produced him to test certain genetic theories of their own before going on to more interesting projects. He'd been pushed hard for the first few years by both parents, then left in the hands of tutors and nannies. He thought of them as teeth, hands and eyes, and for years he'd had bad dreams about a particularly stern individual who had ruled his life until he was seven, when he'd been fortunate enough to escape to boarding school.

At the age of thirteen he'd taken his first degree, but when it came to peer relationships, he hadn't even left the cradle. After a few painful and unsuccessful attempts to fit in, he'd given up trying. His work had benefited, though his personality and disposition had suffered.

Periodically, Hattie, his only other relative, would drag him off to a decent barber and a haberdasher, then fling him in the direction of some hapless female of her acquaintance, hoping nature would take its course.

He'd hoped so, too. God knows, he didn't enjoy being a hermit, and the only thirty-two-year-old male virgin extant.

For that matter, he couldn't even swear he was still a virgin, which only made matters worse. Oh, he had all the right inclinations, there was no doubt of that. But at the thought of doing anything about it, he invariably froze up and broke out in a cold sweat. Even if he'd been given the opportunity, he very much doubted that he'd have been able to rise to the occasion.

It was much simpler to avoid temptation. Not that it came his way too often. Now and then one of the newer female members of the staff would make an overture, but lately even that had ceased. He wasn't a particularly handsome man. His hair was too short, his glasses too thick, and he seemed to have developed a perpetual scowl somewhere along the line, probably from years spent hunched over a book or peering into things that bored the hell out of every woman he'd ever met outside the lab.

So he'd stopped trying. He'd let his beard grow, given up on the idea of trading in his glasses for contacts and accepted his fate. Periodically Malvern would remind him to get a haircut, and he always had it cut extra short so that he wouldn't have to go so often. Hattie deplored it. Personally, Clem considered it remarkably efficient for a man who had never been notably practical.

"There's got to be a woman somewhere who can speak your language," Hattie had cried in exasperation when her last effort had failed. It had been doomed from the start.

The woman, a potter, had been even more shy than he was, and she'd smelled like mildew.

"Give up, Hattie," he'd told her. "I can't dance with them, I can't talk to them—I haven't seen a film in years, and I didn't understand the last few I saw. I'm content the way I am. Why ruin an evening for some perfectly nice woman?"

"It's a waste, and I never could abide the waste of good raw material," Hattie had grumbled. "One of these days you'll fall in love, and then you'll wish you'd got in a bit of practice instead of wasting all your time in that stinky old laboratory."

Hattie had been married four times and had had numerous affairs, or so she claimed. "You're the romantic in the family, Aunt Hattie. If only you weren't my relative, I'd steal you away from your potting and painting and meddling," he'd once teased.

The funny thing was, he'd always been perfectly articulate with Hattie while he hadn't spoken more than a dozen words to his mother, a renowned physicist, in years. And with all other women, he was a total basket case.

Another phone call came the next day. Clement had just taught himself the fine art of rappeling, and was daubing an antiseptic cream on an assortment of scrapes and cuts. He let the answering machine take over. Having given up on hearing from Malvern or Hattie, he preferred to minimize the risk of having to converse with a stranger, and some of Hattie's friends were pretty strange.

It was the same woman, and she sounded, if anything, even more harried than the last time. "Look, Hattie—oh, drat this machine! I hate talking blind, but I know how much you hate to stop what you're doing to answer the phone. Anyway, this man I told you about? Well, I can't take it another day. He just won't quit, and I've told him—Oh, Lordy, here he comes!''

For a long time, Clement sat on the Turkish leather ottoman and pondered this latest message, his long legs sprawled across the dusty parquet floor. There was a considerably higher stress level this time. Whoever the woman was, she was really frightened. Of what? A man. What man? Why was she frightened? Was it because of something the man had done, or something she had done?

The small puzzle, on which he would never, under ordinary circumstances, have wasted a second thought, engaged his mind all through dinner, which consisted of sliced pineapple and Brunswick stew, eaten directly from the cans. Dishwashing was not one of his major accomplishments. There was a machine, but it was obscenely noisy and seemed wasteful for one person.

As for cooking, he could manage if he absolutely had to, but he preferred not to bother. There was a country store with a good supply of canned goods within comfortable hiking distance. He wouldn't starve.

The next call came the following morning just as he stepped out of the shower. Not bothering to dress as he was alone in the house, Clem sat on the foot of the bed and waited.

It was much like the others. She was frightened. She was wondering why Hattie hadn't once answered the phone, if she'd forgotten inviting her. She thought perhaps she should forget about visiting now and go on home.

''Yes, please,'' Clem muttered at the dusty black instrument. He was glad she'd decided not to come—otherwise he might have had to pick up the receiver and actually speak to her. He racked his mind for a clue as to who Hattie might have invited to visit, but if she'd been expecting a visitor, she had forgotten about it and forgotten to warn him, as well.

The last thing he needed was to have some semihysterical woman show up on his doorstep.

After an invigorating hike into town for milk and eggs, Clem tackled his daily stint of wood chopping. It was really rather surprising how quickly he'd taken to the unaccustomed physical regime. The only subject he'd ever done poorly on was physical education. Not the theoretical part, but the rest of it. He'd suffered from asthma as a child, and by the time he'd outgrown that, he'd shot up so that he was all uncoordinated limbs. Add to that a lack of motivation and an extreme astigmatism and it was no wonder he hadn't turned out to be a star athlete.

He took off his shirt—he'd brought along half a dozen, and he'd somehow managed to split a seam or pop a few buttons on each. Positioning the chunk of pine on its end, he lifted the ax over his head and brought it down in the exact center. The two halves fell apart, and he shoved them aside with his foot and reached for another section of firewood.

Martha glanced over her shoulder and spoke quickly into the phone, dismayed to find herself connected to the answering machine again. She was beginning to believe she'd dreamed up Hattie and the invitation to visit her on her way from Louisville to Winston-Salem. Darn it, if she weren't so anxious to get away without being followed, she'd forget the whole thing and go directly to Winston.

"Hattie, this sort of thing just doesn't *happen* to people like me. You probably think I'm imagining the whole thing, but I assure you I'm not. Look, if you're there, I'm coming as soon as I can get away without being followed, and if you're not, I'm probably coming anyway because I don't know what else to do. So if it's not convenient, then I'm sorry. You should answer your phone now and then so people would know what to plan on.''

Hanging up the phone, she peered through the sparse crowd at Mack and Ida's Truck Stop. He was still there, pretending to be interested in a display of the owner's bowling trophies.

The creep! If Jack were here, he'd—

No, he wouldn't. Her brother Jack was many things, but foolhardy he was not. He'd likely tell her she was imagining the whole thing and he'd probably be right. Either that or he'd tell her to hand over her emerald and get on with finding herself a job and a place to stay. Again, he'd be right.

Briefly she considered asking one of the drivers at the counter for a ride into Winston. Or anyplace where she could catch a bus. But at this point she was tired and edgy—edgy, nothing, she was just plain scared! And the last thing she wanted to do was to climb into an eighteen wheeler with another stranger. She'd had enough of those.

Hattie was a known quantity. They'd been friends, despite the differences in age and background, since the well-known art teacher had taught a course in watercolor at the Yadkinville Community Center. As soon as Martha had been old enough to drive, she'd taken the truck once a week and driven to Winston to study basic drawing, clay sculpture, landscape and more watercolor. If Hattie taught it, Martha took it. The two of them had developed a lasting friendship that had continued through intermittent letters even after Martha had dropped out of school and gone to Kentucky to look after her brother's children when his wife had died.

Martha had really looked forward to seeing her mentor again, but it was beginning to seem less and less likely. Hattie seemed to have forgotten all about her offer to meet

Martha at the last stop on the tour and drive her to Cat Creek for a few days' visit. Which was rather unfortunate, as she desperately needed a friend at the moment. The trouble was, if she walked into a bus station and bought a ticket for Winston-Salem, Hubert Odwell would be right on her heels. Sooner or later he'd catch up with her, because he was greedy and unscrupulous and he'd obviously pegged her right off for a pushover. He was probably right, too, she thought with a sigh.

Along with twenty-three other amateur rock hounds, Martha climbed aboard the chartered bus, glancing quickly over her shoulder as she mounted the high step. There he was, standing beside his rusty blue sedan picking his teeth as casually as if he hadn't followed them all the way from Hiddenite to Black Mountain, stopping at every site along the way.

He'd claimed to be some sort of an expert, and a few of her fellow tour members had taken their finds to him to be evaluated. Martha hadn't, but only because she was reasonably certain she'd found nothing of any value. Nor was she expecting to. She'd simply been having fun, relaxing for the first time in years.

But that was before she'd found the emerald.

She was beginning to wish she'd never found the darned thing, but she had, and she was too stubborn to give in to that creep! It was just her luck that Odwell had happened to be with her when she'd found it. He'd approached her several times, as he had most of the others, seeming to have a decided preference for women. Maybe he thought they were better gem hunters than men. Or luckier. More gullible, probably.

"Hey, you're not giving up, are you, little lady? I told you most of these places was salted. I'll show you where the good stuff is, I got my car right over there."

"No, thanks, I'll stick with the group. I'm perfectly happy with what I've found." And she was. While once she might have envisioned discovering a fortune in gems—what child living so near the mountains of North Carolina hadn't heard fantastic tales of fabulous sapphires and emeralds plowed up in a field?—she'd long since outgrown that stage. Reality had a way of dulling even the most vivid imagination.

"You give up too easy, little lady. Don't be that way—ol' Hubert can show you a place where you can really strike it rich."

"Look, would you *stop* calling me little lady? And would you stop following me around? Go find the Hope Diamond or something. I've got a headache and I'd like to be left alone!" Normally the most peaceable of women, Martha had been pushed beyond her limit. She'd swung around to confront the man, only to find him right on her heels. To keep from colliding with him, she'd thrown out her arms, and her shoulder bag had slipped off her arm and struck a tree, scattering her belongings in a wide arc.

"Oh, blast! Now look what you made me do!" She'd dropped to her knees on the gravel and leaned over a low barricade. If she'd been ten feet further to the right, she'd have lost everything over a sheer drop. As it was, the contents of her purse had landed in leaf-strewn mud, under scrubby bushes and gnarled roots.

Her wallet was closest, and she'd snatched it and rammed it into her bag. Then she'd begun collecting her address book, her hair brush, sunglasses, Chapstick and an assortment of other paraphernalia. She'd found her tube of tearose hand cream under a witch-hobble plant, her pen caught in a clump of snakeroot and then she'd started searching for the matching mechanical pencil.

Virgil Jones, a man she'd considered herself practically engaged to until two months ago, had given her that set. Not a wildly romantic gift, but then she evidently wasn't the sort to bring out the romantic side of any man. Certainly Virgil hadn't thought so. If she'd been smarter, she might have tumbled earlier to the fact that Virgil hadn't considered her his equal, either mentally, socially or in any other way.

"Need some help?" She'd felt Odwell's hand on her upturned bottom and swung around to glare at him just as her fingers closed around a gritty-feeling cylinder.

"No, thank you," she'd said through clenched teeth. "I've found it. If you want to help me, just go away and leave me alone, will you?" She brushed off her pencil and started to drop it into her purse when it dawned on her that her pencil was much more slender, much smoother—and it had a clip on the side, not an irregular lump.

Slowly, she'd opened her hand. And then she'd gasped. The rock lying across her palm had been a green crystal partially encased in dull matrix, its surface rough and coated with mud. Even so, there'd been no mistaking its brilliant green purity.

"Hey, hold on a minute, what have we got here, honey?" Odwell had moved closer, reaching for her hand. "Looks like we made us a lucky find, don't it?"

Acting instinctively, Martha had shoved the crystal into her purse and clamped the worn leather satchel under her arm. "*We* found nothing. Thanks to you, I lost part of a pen and pencil set that was given to me by someone I—I hold very dear!"

Dear? Since their last disastrous evening together, when he'd told her that she was a nice girl and that she'd make some lucky man a fine housewife—*housewife!*—she'd held Virgil Jones about as dear as she held weevils in the pantry.

"I'll give you ten dollars for it, sight unseen."

"My *pencil*?"

Odwell's pudgy red face had taken on a less genial cast. "Yeah, your pencil, honey. You know what I mean—that chunk of pretty green glass you just hid in your bag."

"Oh, for pity's sake," she'd exclaimed nervously, "it's just a—a souvenir. You don't find emeralds in a parking lot."

"Around these parts, you find 'em most anywhere. And I was with you when you found it, so half of whatever we can get for it belongs to me."

The man was crazy! Edging toward the bus, Martha had watched him warily. "That's ridiculous. Whatever I found—and I'm not saying I found anything, mind you— belongs to me. If you'd seen it and picked it up, I certainly wouldn't—"

"A hundred. That's my top offer, lady, and I'm only doing that because I took a real liking to your looks."

Martha might not be the world's most experienced woman, but she was no fool. Her looks were about as exciting as day-old bread. Average height, average build, average reddish-blond hair, brows and lashes. Her most striking feature was probably the pale brown colour of her eyes, and that only because they matched the million or so freckles that covered every exposed part of her body.

"Huh!" she'd snorted, warily edging toward the door of the bus. That door had better have a lock on the inside, because if it didn't she was going to sit on the horn until someone came to her rescue.

"Just leave me alone, will you? It's nothing!"

"Lemme see. I know minerals, and I can tell if we got ourselves a genu-wine emerald or just a pretty paperweight."

She'd struggled with the door—how the devil did these things work, anyway? And then, to her monumental relief, she'd heard the others converging on the bus, wearily comparing sunburned arms and the results of their afternoon dig.

"Ready to head for the motel?" Oscar, the driver, was a real expert when it came to maneuvering the lumbering bus around hairpin turns, but he wasn't the least bit interested in dirtying his hands in the hopes of finding a fortune in precious gems.

"I'll see you later, honey," Hubert Odwell had promised, and Martha, shivering in earnest, had tried to ignore him.

That was how it had started. She'd waited until her roommate had gone to sleep to call Hattie, but all she'd gotten was the answering machine with her friend's zany instructions. Which hadn't been what she'd needed at that point.

The tour, which had gotten her back to North Carolina from Louisville, Kentucky for half the regular bus fare, thanks to a friend at the travel agency and a last-minute, no-refund cancellation, had been a real pleasure up until then.

And dammit, she hated to be forced to cut short her first real vacation in so many years because of a sleazy character who was probably more of a nuisance than a genuine threat. By tomorrow, she told herself again and again, he'd have forgotten her and latched onto some other poor soul.

Only he hadn't. And seeing that rusty blue sedan turn up at stop after stop had only increased her nervousness.

The tour plan had been to visit eight different mining areas as they worked their way southwest, more or less following the Blue Ridge Mountains but coming down for the most promising locations. Such as the one where she'd found the emerald. The tour was to end in Asheville, where she would have been met by Hattie, and they would have spent a few days together at Hattie's home in what she'd laughingly referred to as the suburbs of Cat Creek.

Only everything was going wrong. First there was Hubert Odwell, and then she'd been unable to reach Hattie. And now she didn't know quite what to do.

Fortunately, Clement's sense of hearing was considerably more acute than his sense of sight. Because he'd lost his glasses again. It happened with depressing regularity whenever he was doing anything active, which was most of the time, lately. Bent over a microscope in a climate-controlled environment, they were perfectly secure, but on a sweating face when he was wielding an ax, nothing was safe.

The vehicle, whatever it was, was barely up to the strain of such a steep grade, from the sound of it. Tires slid on gravel, and he could hear pebbles striking a surface far below the road—a drop of some hundred or so meters.

The road ended at this place, so it couldn't be a passerby. Which could mean only one thing—Hattie was home. Praise Paracelsus! As much as he'd enjoyed it, he wasn't sure he could survive much longer. Considering he'd never even been to summer camp, it was a wonder he'd managed to do as well as he had.

Which had no doubt been the whole point of Hattie's experiment.

The truck stopped directly in front of the house, disgorging a single passenger. Either that or the pink wraith that moved away from the large white vehicle was a ghost, and while, scientist or not, Clement didn't dismiss anything as impossible, he rather hoped it would turn out to be the corporeal entity of his great-aunt.

Shirtless, ax in hand, he made his way cautiously as far as he dared. "Hattie?"

Unfortunately, the truck roared off at that moment, and her reply was lost. She was obviously waiting for him to fetch her luggage, but he didn't dare go forth, not until she'd helped him locate his spectacles. He'd slid down too many embankments, tripped on too many rocks and roots to risk moving far in his present condition. "I was beginning to wonder if you'd deserted me altogether. I'll get your luggage if you'll find my glasses for me. I think they're over near the woodpile."

Again her answer was lost in the noise of the departing truck—a delivery van of some sort, from the shape of it. "How was Greece? By the way, you're expecting a visitor. She called several times, and I gather she'll be arriving any time now. Thank God you're back, because if I had to deal with this weirdo, I'd probably end up crawling into that hole in the ground you call your kiln."

The dim figure at the far edge of his vision hadn't moved. Nor had she spoken. Or if she had, Clement hadn't heard her. That was when it occurred to him that something was definitely out of kilter here. If she wasn't a ghost and she wasn't Hattie, then the only other person he could think of who might be arriving on this forsaken slab of rock was— was...

Oh, God, not her. Not some hysterical female stranger, and him not even able to see her! He could feel the hair on his arms prickle as his skin tightened. Every muscle in his body contracted. In fact, contracted with considerably more efficiency than many of them had ever manifested in the past. All those hours spent climbing, hiking and wood chopping had evidently reconstructed him to a certain extent, at least physically.

But he was still so much dead meat when it came to actually interacting with a strange woman. She would have to go. That was all there was to it, because he wasn't up to dealing with her, and he damned well wasn't up to explaining why!

"Hattie, where the devil are you?" he muttered under his breath.

Hefting the ax, Clem started toward the fuzzy pink figure, feeling his way cautiously over the rough terrain. The sooner they reached an understanding as to who was going and who was staying, the better he would like it. He'd been feeling pretty good about himself, all things considered, and then she'd had to come along and ruin it.

Two

Martha stared uncertainly at the tall, bearded man in the rumpled white pants. His bare chest was patterned with dark hair, as were his arms. He had large, capable-looking hands. One of which happened to be holding an ax.

Her pulse tripped into double time. Drawing a deep, calming breath, she glanced at the cloud of dust thrown up by the bread truck that was roaring off down the grade. If there was still the slightest chance of catching it . . .

There wasn't. She turned to face the bearded stranger. "What have you done wi— Where's Hattie? Oh, no, you don't!" She held up a hand, palm outward. "Not one step closer, do you hear me? I'm not kidding. I've got a voice like a fire siren, and I promise you, I'll scream if you . . ." She swallowed hard.

The stranger held his ground, his face—or as much of it as she could see—expressionless. There was something about him—about the way he was looking at her. As if he

(partially obscured text under folded corner)

and buried under a layer of tea-rose talcum po
could dash past him, snatch it and—
To heck with her emerald. She could m
cumbered. With a lot of luck and a h
even be able to outrun him, althoug
long and looked uncomfortably
slouch—she hadn't spent th
with a pair of hyperactiv
"Er, um . . . mumbl
and Martha took a
a bed of small
"Where'
"You'
"I

(left column, partially obscured)

f
bu
co

I
hav
this

Sh
the co
didn't
she sai
if tryin
blowgu

Oh, g
Nikes.

Clemen ... ognized the fact
that the p ... terrified of something, and
that bothe ... Had the man who was terrorizing her
followed her here? He hadn't noticed anyone else, but there
could've been an army out there, and as long as they remained silent, he would never know it.

She needed reassurance. He could offer her that much, at
least. "You're safe here. Come closer."

"Uh, no, thanks. I think I'll just mosey on back down the
mountain and call Hattie later on. She's obviously busy on
some project or other—all I've been getting is her answering machine." Martha's eyes widened as the man took a
shambling step toward her. He was roughly the size of a
telephone booth, and for all his soft, oddly hesitant voice,
there was nothing soft or hesitant about that ax. She glanced
at her toilet case, which was perched precariously atop her
battered old suitcase. Her emerald was wrapped in a tissue

vder. She

ove faster unen-
ad start, she might
n those legs of his were
powerful. Still, she was no
e past three years keeping up
youngsters for nothing.

e, mumble, mumble," said the man,
step backward and felt her foot slide on
ebbles.

Hattie?" she challenged once more.
re the same one. You're still frightened."
am not," she denied automatically. Boldly, she met his
yes, hoping to intimidate him into backing off. Before she realized it, she was caught. Trapped by—by what? A pair of blue eyes? She'd seen blue eyes before, she scoffed.

Yes, but never that sparkly, intense shade of blue. And never with that deep-set quality of—

Of what? Vulnerability? That was ridiculous! She'd never seen a less vulnerable man in her life.

"Yes," the blue-eyed man said calmly, and she scrambled desperately to remember what they'd been talking about. "It was fear I heard in your voice each time. It's still there."

All right, so she was a bit uneasy and he knew it. That couldn't be helped. His own voice was certainly calm enough. Deep and quiet, and sort of...hmm. It was only her imagination that made it sound like the sort of voice Virgil called "cultured." The word had always reminded her of buttermilk.

Okay, so maybe there was a brain cell under all that hair. The brightest ones were sometimes the first to go sailing off the deep end. Even those from the very best families, like that case in the news just last month. In spite of what Virgil claimed, money, education and breeding were no guarantee of anything except membership in a few stodgy clubs.

Clement could feel her uneasiness, even though he couldn't see it. He ventured a step closer, then another one, because she was standing entirely too close to the far side of the drive. "Hattie's in—uh, she's still in Greece," he said, thankful he had taken time to familiarize himself with this portion of the property. "I thought you were she. That is, I thought the truck was Hattie. I mean, mumble, mumble, mumble."

Exhaling, he felt a trickle of sweat form in the hollow of his cheek just below the beard line. He shoved a hand roughly through his hair, leaving one dark shock to flop forward onto his brow.

Actually, he was doing pretty well, considering that he couldn't see more than a foot beyond the tip of his nose. He'd sounded almost coherent there for a minute, too. Evidently, his social skills had improved right along with his physical prowess.

"You know Hattie Davenport?" She sounded almost suspicious.

"Great-nephew. Paternal grandmother's—um, sister. You know."

The blur became a bit less blurred as he moved a step closer. He halted. While he was increasingly curious as to her looks, he had always preferred that his personal space remain inviolate. Unfortunately, handicapped as he was by his temporary lack of vision, he might be forced to compromise.

The woman stepped back again, much too close to the edge of the drop, and Clem braced himself for what must be done. Personal space or no, he could hardly allow her to fall off the mountain. Besides, he needed to see who he was dealing with. If he ever located his glasses again he was going to weld the damned things onto his head! He couldn't see to split wood without them, but as soon as he worked up a sweat, they slid off.

"You mentioned losing your glasses?" the woman said, and he wondered if she were telepathic. Testing him for weakness, more likely. He had mentioned having lost his glasses when he'd thought she was Hattie.

A sloucher by habit, Clem drew himself up to his full six feet four, frowning in the general direction of the pink wraith. Why was she testing him? Surely she didn't distrust him. He didn't expect her to be drawn to him, but any fool could see that he was perfectly harmless.

Squinting against the late-afternoon glare, he did what had to be done. "Barto. C. Cornelius Barto."

That should settle matters quickly enough. His latest piece on bipolarization of mutagens had come out just last month in the *Hastings Quarterly*, and before that there'd been that paper on the philosophic rationalization for biogenetic engineering. Clement had never been one to boast of his accomplishments, but if this woman didn't recognize his credentials, his obvious respectability, then it was up to him to enlighten her.

No response. Not a word. All right, so perhaps she'd missed it. Some people's taste in reading matter—Hattie's, for instance—didn't run to scientific journals. "Well?" he demanded. It was her turn now. Who was she? How long was she planning to stay?

She took another step back, and Clem, with uncharacteristic impatience and total disregard for any possible danger, acted. Praying he wouldn't trip on the rock-ribbed, root-threaded terrain, he lunged forward and slung the ax around behind her, cutting off her retreat.

Over his own accelerated heartbeat, he could hear the erratic sound of her breathing. A series of small, shallow gasps, then nothing.

Thunder rumbled in the distance. A wren scolded noisily. A gust of wind stirred the dust, sending down a shower of colorful confetti from various deciduous trees. Clement was oblivious to everything except for the woman he was holding pressed against him with the flat side of his ax. His nostrils flared as he drew in her scent. Faintly sweet, faintly spicy, it was a vaguely familiar scent. It smelled . . . warm.

The scientist in him shuddered at the crossing of sensory data, while another part of him, a part he scarcely recognized, stirred, sat up and began to examine the infinite possibilities of such a mixture.

Reaching up, his hand struck a bit of warm, firm flesh and hung on. He recognized the delicate shape of humerus, clavicle and scapula and closed his fingers firmly over her shoulder. She was rigid. Paralyzed with...fear? Dear Lord, what did she think he was going to do to her, bite off her head? He'd probably saved her life.

"Exhale," he ordered, and she did, in a long, shuddering gust. "Now inhale." She gasped. "Slowly!" he barked, and gradually her breathing began to level out. "That's better. Now turn your head to the light so that I can see you better."

He leaned closer, until his nose was practically touching hers. Until he could see the widening of pale amber eyes surrounded by remarkably dense gold-tipped copper lashes. The sclera was clear, almost blue-white. While he watched, her pupils began to contract, then quickly expanded until all but a rim of the iris was hidden.

Hmm, interesting response, he thought with slightly less than clinical objectivity. Considerably more distracted than usual, Clem, through force of habit, set about cataloging the remaining physical data before him. If the thought occurred to him that his reaction was totally out of character, he dismissed it. Personal space forgotten, he clutched her shoulder, holding her pressed against him with the ax as he attempted to assay her face.

Only gradually did he become aware of the soft mewing sound issuing from her throat. He wasn't hurting her. Hands that could hold a butterfly without ruffling a wing would never hurt a woman. All the same, he took care.

How exciting were the complex curves of a woman's facial structure. Far less angular than his own. And not only her facial structure, for he was becoming increasingly aware of her *femaleness* pressing against him. A certain softness in the mammary region . . . the distinctive conformation of the pelvic girdle . . .

Suddenly, Clem stiffened. To his dismay, his mind wasn't the only part of him that noticed the difference. His body was starting to react with rather amazing enthusiasm. Praise Paracelsus! What a time to get—what was that term he'd heard recently?—turned on. He was struck with remorse when he noticed her eyes widening with panic.

"Please," she whispered.

Frantically, he sought the words to reassure her. "Oh. Yes. That is . . . yes," he stammered. Still holding her with one hand, he dropped the ax. They were mere inches from the edge. He'd paced off the distance in case of just such an occurrence as this.

"No, not precisely like this," he qualified in a distracted murmur. Clement often spoke his thoughts aloud. Or fragments of those thoughts. No one, to his knowledge, had ever been frightened by the sound of his voice before.

The woman trembling under his hands was obviously terrified. "Would you please let me go?" she whispered.

"I'll leave right now, and I promise you, I won't tell anyone where you are. I *promise*."

Clement frowned. Nothing she'd said made sense. Leaving was impractical, and revealing his presence here was irrelevant. Fear, he supposed, could manifest itself as confusion. Solicitously, he drew her away from the edge of the drop, allowing one hand to linger comfortably on her arm. Her biceps were slender, but surprisingly firm. How remarkable—he would have thought that biceps would be genderless, but hers felt decidedly female.

On a subliminal level, Clement was aware that he was reacting in a thoroughly unscientific way to this unexpected stimulus. "I gave you my name. You didn't."

"My name? It's M—Martha. Eberly."

Of course. She'd given her name when she'd called, but he'd been more interested in the quality of her voice than in her identity. "Martha," he repeated, testing the feel of it on his tongue. He decided it was a fine name, a womanly name, and was unaware of having reacted in a completely unscientific manner. "Come inside, Martha. The water's cold."

Martha stood her ground, her eyes never leaving his. Dimly, she remembered hearing something about not looking a strange dog directly in the eyes, but she couldn't help herself. His were mesmerizing.

However, if he thought he was going to drown her, he was sadly mistaken. She hadn't escaped from Hubert Odwell only to let herself fall into the hands of some overgrown fruitcake with wild-blue-yonder eyes and dubious intentions. "Yes, of course—inside. You go first and I'll follow just as soon as I get my things," she said in her best Aunt-Marty-knows-best tone of voice.

What she'd follow was that bread truck—and so fast he wouldn't see her for the dust! What had he called himself?

C. Cornelius Something-or-Other? Powerfully pompous
name for such a ragtag looking creature. And while he might
not be precisely balmy, she wasn't about to hang around
long enough to find out what his problem was. Any man
who came at her with an ax, even if he only used it to keep
her from falling off a mountain, was definitely not her first
choice for a companion.

Never mind that sexy voice of his that for one split second had made her insides curl up and purr. Never mind that
for a single, solitary moment, she'd had the wildest urge to
throw herself into those naked, sweaty arms and beg shelter from steep cliffs, sleazy con men and all the rest of life's
miserable little surprises. Martha *knew* what her problem
was, and C. Cornelius What's-it was definitely not the solution.

While she was making up her mind how best to slip past
him, he turned away, tripped over her bags, then, after
apologizing to thin air, swung them up as if both were full
of feathers. Her big bag alone weighed a ton. She'd
crammed it with practically everything she owned, except
for her summer things, which were being shipped as soon as
she had an address. As for her toilet case, it was mostly filled
with rocks. She'd kept every tiny, drab pebble from every
bucket of dirt she'd bought over the past two days, dumping them in with her toothbrush, her curling iron and an
unopened bag of disposable razors. Not to mention her box
of tea-rose scented talcum powder, which just happened to
conceal her ticket to future security.

C. C. What's-his-name smiled at her. At least she hoped
it was a smile. Hiding behind all those wild whiskers, it
could easily have been a grimace.

"Come," he ordered.

Come? As in, me Tarzan, you Jane? Marty stifled a nervous urge to giggle. Really, this whole thing was turning into

a farce. Ax or no, the poor man really did seem harmless
enough. He was probably just some weird eccentric—Hattie had always attracted unusual people. Granted, he'd
scared the socks off her, but he hadn't actually hurt her, and
goodness knows he'd had every opportunity. He could've
shoved her off the cliff or chopped her up into itty-bitty
pieces, but he hadn't. All he'd done was to hold her too
closely and stare at her as if he'd never seen a woman before. She knew she wasn't looking her best today, but did he
have to look at her that way?

Warily, she began to follow him across the graveled road
that curved around to end at a pair of closed garage doors.
Dead end. No through traffic. Probably no traffic at all, she
thought sinkingly, as hope of hitching a ride out of here began to fade.

Stumbling over an exposed rock, she recovered herself
and continued to follow him, not knowing what else to do
at this point. She no longer deluded herself into thinking she
could run all the way down the mountain. It was late in the
day—the sun would have set before she'd got halfway to the
main road, and she had no real desire to be walking along
the narrow shoulder of one of these twisting mountain
blacktops after dark.

Halfway across the steep, wooded yard, she put a hand to
her temple and rubbed absently. It was tension, pure tension. No wonder her head hurt. It was just a wonder that
was all that hurt.

Come to think of it, it wasn't, but the backache was
something she'd brought on herself, leaning over all those
buckets of dirt. When she'd thought about rock hunting,
she'd always pictured herself using a chisel and hammer or
picking up dazzling gems in clear mountain streams. Not
pawing through buckets full of gritty mud.

Glasses or no, C. Cornelius was as surefooted as a mountain goat, Martha thought sourly. Slogging tiredly along several yards behind him, she frowned at the way his lower back flexed with each step, like a well-oiled bronze machine. There was a tiny patch of dark hair just above his dirty white pants on either side of his spine and a shadow where his spine disappeared under his waistband.

And then her gaze migrated a few inches downward. He must know those pants of his were indecently snug. Evidently he thought he was giving her a treat. Hmph! She wouldn't give those seams of his much of a chance if he bent over too many times!

It occurred to her that she was indulging in precisely what she'd often accused her friend Linda at the travel agency of doing. Man watching. Of all the ridiculous things—she must be slightly hysterical. Linda would've liked this one. Great buns, she would've said. A real hunk, hair and all.

Frankly, Martha had always preferred a few brains and a modicum of manners, but then, look where it had got her.

He was getting ahead of her. "Hold on, there, where are you going with my bags?" He was halfway up the stone steps, halfway to the wide, gingerbread porch that was guarded by a pair of mossy concrete gargoyles. She challenged him. "Well?"

Lowering her bags to the steps, he said, "Inside."

"I never said I was staying. Where's Hattie?"

"I told you—Greece."

"What if I don't believe you? Maybe this isn't even her house. Maybe you aren't who you said you were. How do I know?"

He came down the steps, stopping on the bottom one. "It is. I am. Where will you go?"

Her shoulders slumped. Where indeed? It was late—soon it would be dark. Not to mention cold. She was miles from civilization and she didn't know a single soul west of Winston-Salem, which was at least three hours away, even if she'd had the means to get there. And to top it off, Hubert Odwell could already have discovered that she was no longer on the bus and be doubling back, asking around.

"All right, but just for tonight," she said grudgingly.

He didn't smile, he didn't speak, he didn't do anything but stare. Marty armed herself with a description in case it became necessary later on. Tall. *Really* tall and bearded, of course, his hair probably lighter than it looked because it was wet with sweat. Dark brown, she'd call it, not black. His clothes, such as they were, were filthy. He needed a bath, too, because there were dirt stains on his arms.

On the other hand, he'd smelled clean enough. In fact, there was something quite pleasant about the way he smelled. Like whatever all those evergreen trees were—sort of resiny, crisp and masculine.

Oh, boy, she was *really* losing her grip! "I'm not sure this is a good idea," she hedged. "I mean, if Hattie isn't even home, maybe I'd better come back some other time." Plastering what she hoped was a convincing smile on her face, she waited for him to offer to drive her to the nearest bus station.

"You'll get wet."

On the point of wondering if the man had a water fixation, Marty heard a crack of thunder that seemed to echo forever. He'd known it was going to rain. These primitive types could probably smell it. And while she still didn't feel any too good about entrusting herself to a stranger—especially a nonverbal, ax-swinging, half naked stranger—she honestly didn't know what else she could do at this point. Maybe he really was a relative of Hattie's. He was probably all right, she told herself in an attempt at reassurance. A bit off the wall, but perfectly safe. Hattie was slightly flaky, but she'd never have gone off and left her home in the care of someone she didn't trust.

A great-nephew? Maybe, maybe not. Hattie had mentioned a nephew once, someone important at Cal Tech. And of course there was the boy whose portrait she'd painted years and years ago. Martha had had a monumental crush on that portrait the summer she was—what? Fifteen? Sixteen? Thereabouts, at least. She could still get a rush just thinking about it, or she would have if she hadn't been so darned tired.

"Well?" she demanded, shifting her weight to the other foot.

"Yes?"

He wasn't going to give an inch. Maybe English wasn't his first language. Maybe he—oh, what the hell! "Okay, I'm stuck here for tonight, but first thing tomorrow, I'm calling a cab."

Thank the Lord for that emerald. She had a hunch she might need it to get her out of hock after this miserable adventure.

Clement smiled. He wasn't a smiler by nature, but he'd thought it might put her at ease. "Coffee," he said. She'd decided to come inside. Good. Because he couldn't very well have left her outside, and he hadn't the slightest notion of how to get her moving again.

"You said the magic word," she told him in the voice he'd once thought of as breathless. It was more of a huskiness— an uncertain quality. Just as Clem was leading the way up the old stone steps lightning split the sky, and he hastened to reassure her. "Lightning rods."

"I know, Hattie sent me a picture when she first moved up here. I thought the house looked like a wedding cake."

"No, it's a house."

"I didn't mean it literally," she said dryly.

"Oh. Yes."

Actually, with a bath, some decent clothes and a marathon session with a barber, he wouldn't be half bad, she told herself as he let her into a rather gloomy foyer, with a curving stairway on one side and a velvet-draped arch on the other. However, if he could provide her with a cup of coffee and a place to catch her breath until she could find a way to get out of here, he could shave his head and wear a hula skirt for all she cared.

"I have food, too."

"How nice," she said with a weak smile. She would humor him. He was trying to offer hospitality.

"You can sleep in my bed."

"Whoa! Hold it right there, friend." Poor Hattie. If this really was one of her nephews, no wonder she'd kept the poor soul under wraps. He was certainly nothing like the one in the portrait. Hattie had once described that one as a gentle soul who was too brainy for his own good and misunderstood by most ordinary people. Martha had had to hide an overwhelming desire to snatch up the portrait and shield it from a cold, cruel world. The feeling had persisted even after she'd learned that the subject had an I.Q. that rivaled the national debt and was stashed away in a brain trust somewhere up north.

"Um—sleep," she said. "Well, really, maybe I'll just have a cup of coffee and be on my way." Fine, just great, but where? How?

"Hattie's room is closed. Damp. I don't mind damp."

Ushering her inside, Clement heard his guest exhale noisily. He'd forgotten the altitude. While it wasn't all that high, some people might find it a problem, particularly if they came from somewhere near sea level. "Seashore?" he asked.

"See *what*?"

For two cents he would give up trying to communicate with her. She was evidently no better at it than he was. Strange woman, he mused, setting her luggage on the stair landing. But then, what did he know about women? Perhaps they were all strange, and he'd just never noticed. It wouldn't be the first time he'd completely overlooked the obvious while in pursuit of the obscure.

"Water first? It's ice cold. High in mineral content, but harmless. Or coffee? Without my glasses, I don't do that very well, but there's food."

By George, he was becoming positively garrulous! He only hoped she wouldn't be bored by all this chattering. Personally, he was rather impressed with himself.

Martha. Martha Eberly. Interesting arrangement of syllables. But the most remarkable thing of all was that something about this woman was bringing out a whole new facet of his personality, one he had never suspected he possessed. A savoir faire, so to speak.

Clem smiled broadly, feeling happy, relaxed and closer to confident than he ever remembered feeling outside his own territory. "Sit," he said. "You can read labels. Wait right here—don't go away, I'll be right back."

Read labels?

He was back in less than a minute, his arms loaded with cans. Some he could recognize by the shape—the canned ham and sardines. But Martha Eberly might not care for sardines. Perhaps she'd prefer the pâté. There were crackers somewhere that were probably not too stale.

Perhaps the crab soup with sherry... "There's wine to drink," he remembered suddenly. "I don't know about what goes with what. I seldom bother." He never bothered unless he was out with Hattie, and then she selected, but only after a long discussion with the wine steward, which, often as not, ended in that gentleman's agreeing to sit for her.

With a smile, his second in mere minutes—gad, he must be delirious!—Clem dumped the lot onto an inlaid walnut table and waited for her to choose. A guest for dinner. *His* guest! By damn, but he liked the sound of that. Last year he'd invited a visiting biophysicist to an awards dinner, but she'd preferred to attend alone. So had he, actually. It had taken him more than a week to get up his nerve to ask, and he'd only done it because Ed Malvern, his secretary, had implied that, as senior member of the team, it was his duty.

But this was different. Never once had he considered entertaining a woman in his home. He maintained a small apartment near B.F.I., but he spent very little time there, as there was a comfortable cot in his office, a shower adjoining his lab and food and drink machines in the basement.

Standing awkwardly beside the table, he continued to wait, occasionally shifting his weight from one foot to the other. He rammed his hands into his pockets and then took them out again; crossed his arms and then uncrossed them. He'd give anything to be able to see her. She hadn't spoken a word. Was she waiting for him to tell her what to do?

It was too dark! "More light?" he asked eagerly, and switched on a tassled floor lamp. "If you don't see anything you like, I could, um, go to the grocers. Only he closes at six, and it's a four-mile walk."

"Don't you have a car?"

"I don't drive."

"You don't drive?" She sounded amazed.

"I learned once. I had little natural aptitude."

"That doesn't usually stop people."

Clem considered her words and found that he concurred. Hattie, for instance, could barely see over the dashboard, and she was constantly using her hands to talk when she drove, pointing out landscapes she'd like to paint.

The silence stretched out uncomfortably while Clement waited for Martha to tell him what she wanted to eat. He stroked his beard. Beards, he had discovered, had their uses, one of which was to provide a barrier behind which to hide. Just now, his was also providing an outlet for nervous energy.

Was she waiting for something? Was it his turn to speak? He'd made a statement; they'd concurred; end of discussion. As there was still one outstanding question on the table, the next move was hers. If she didn't make it, he hadn't the faintest idea of what to do or say next.

"Do you need to use the bathroom?" A stroke of genius, he prided himself. Just when the conversation had begun to languish.

"What? Oh—please."

She got to her feet. He could see her shape, her color, shades of pink, coppery on top and paler down below. Pink feet.

"Well? Do you have a tourist map, or am I on my own?"

Clement seldom recognized sarcasm. This time, he did. Whereas, ordinarily, it wouldn't have bothered him, again this time it did. "I'm sorry. I'll show you," he said with all the dignity he could muster, which was considerably more than he knew.

He took her arm. He was not a toucher—never had been. Nor had he been the recipient of many touches, other than inadvertent ones. He was conscious of a strange, prickling sensation that spread from the small area where his hand came in contact with her arm. He wasn't at all sure what caused it—even less sure if he liked it. It felt as if it might be dangerous if allowed to continue unchecked.

"How much can you see without your glasses?"

They were passing through a dining room that looked like a cross between a studio and a flea market. Clement made his way easily, being familiar with the hazards. "Considering the degree of refraction necessary to—"

"I'm not interested in degrees or refractions, I only wanted to know if you're totally blind or not. I hate to go off and leave you here alone if you're really helpless. Don't you have another pair of glasses?"

"No, I'm not. And yes, I do, but they're back in Winston-Salem in my office."

They came to a halt before a door near the back of a narrow hallway. "Can't you send for them?"

"Yes."

"Well, have you?" He detected exasperation in her tone and wondered why his lack of vision should matter to her.

"No."

One hand on the painted china doorknob, Martha stared at him, wondering if he were deliberately trying to tie her brain into knots. Was it some kind of psycho thing he was pulling? "Is it that you *can't* talk, or that you just don't choose to? Listen, C. Cornelius Thingamabob, or whoever you claim to be, I'm too tired to play your childish little games. This was supposed to be my vacation—well, sort of, anyway. And for days all I've done is ride in smelly, noisy buses, dig in buckets full of dirt and sleep in crummy motels with a woman in the next bed who snores like a freight train. I haven't eaten since yesterday, and my head hurts, and I don't care who you are or what you've done, just leave me alone!"

Dead silence reigned for perhaps a full minute. Martha wondered if he were going to kill her on the spot or wait until she'd washed some of the road dust off her face and hands. And then he began to speak, and she could have curled up and died unassisted.

"I'm sorry. Yes, I can talk, but I'm not very good at it. The problem is partially genetic, partially environmental, I suspect. It's too late to do much about it now. I—I'm sorry, Martha. Tell me what I can do to make you comfortable, and I'll do it and then get out of your way. Eat. Stay the night. Stay as long as you like. I won't bother you again."

Three

———

Martha stayed in the bathroom as long as she dared. She eyed the sleek, putty-colored shower unit longingly, wishing she could step inside and let the water flow over her body until all her worries and all the dirt she'd collected from traveling dusty roads at breakneck speed swirled away together down the drain.

Instead, she finger-combed her hair and sleeked the front away from her face with damp hands. Neat but not gaudy, she summed up. That had been her mother's highest accolade. Martha had worn gingham and starched pinafores when every other child in her class had worn jeans. She'd had her face scrubbed raw the first time she'd dared smear on a daub of lipstick, and after that she'd had the good sense to wait until she got to school to paint her face.

Neat but not gaudy. Ignoring the mirror, she dried her hands. Neat she could manage pretty well, at least on most occasions. As for gaudy, that was still her secret ambition, but at the moment she'd settle for neat.

Outside the bathroom, which Hattie had enlarged from a tiny powder room, Clement waited for his guest to emerge. He'd promised to leave her alone, and he would, but first he needed to show her where he'd put her bags.

"Upstairs," he said the minute the door opened.

"Who? What?"

"Um—your bags. Hattie's room. I lit a fire."

"A *fire*?"

He could actually feel her fear, and in his eagerness to re-assure her, Clement reached out and caught at her arms—or what he hoped were her arms. One hand brushed against something remarkably soft, but the contact was so fleeting there was no time to evaluate the other properties of the surface.

"Don't touch me!"

Perplexed by her strange attitude, Clem stepped back. "No. I won't." He heard her sniff.

"A fire?" she repeated.

"Fireplaces. Two upstairs. Living room and dining room downstairs. Same chimney. And the kitchen goes up—" He was talking too much. God, why couldn't he learn to say what he meant and shut up, instead of garbling the information and then tripping over his clumsy feet trying to re-capitulate?

"You lit a fire in the fireplace in Hattie's room," Martha interpreted. She moved away from him. "For me? Thank you."

"I—um, it's too soft. The bed, that is. You're not very padded—pressure points, I mean. But if you'd rather..."

"It'll be just fine," Martha assured him, anxious to reach a room with a door she could shut and lock. As blind as he was—and she was pretty sure he wasn't lying about that—he could hardly see to find his ax. And if she dragged something heavy up against the door from the inside, there was no reason she shouldn't have a good night's sleep before she started looking for a way back to civilization. She'd hardly slept at all since she'd found that darned emerald.

Clement allowed her to go first, and she could feel his eyes on her backside all the way up the stairs. Whether he could see or not, she'd be willing to bet he was staring holes in her. Her spine stiffened and she was extra careful not to wiggle her hips.

"First one on the right," he said in that oddly attractive voice. "I closed it. Um, to keep the heat in."

And she would close it to keep possible intruders *out*. She might be stuck here for the night, but come morning she was going to find her way back to *somewhere* if she had to roll downhill all the way. Hubert Odwell or no Hubert Odwell. C. Cornelius or no C. Cornelius. Evidently Hattie was not quite as sharp as she'd been four or five years ago. It was a bit disconcerting, to say the least, to arrive for an invited visit only to discover that her hostess had forgotten all about inviting her and gone traipsing off to Greece.

Her bags were just inside the door and seemingly intact, but the room itself was a shocker. Along with a small tile-faced fireplace, a square four-poster that sagged like a hammock and an armoire that could easily have housed a small family, there were paintings from floor to ceiling. All styles, all periods and all levels of expertise. Including the portrait of Hattie's brainy great-nephew, which made her catch her breath. She stared at it for a long time before looking away. After all these years, it still had the ability to make her feel soft and trembly inside. Hattie had to be immensely talented as a painter, because Martha was not a soft and trembly sort of woman.

A connecting door revealed another bath, this one re-plete with a lovely bathtub encased in golden oak. Unfor-tunately she wouldn't be staying around long enough to enjoy it.

Two hours later Martha huddled in the center of the massive bed, wondering how she was going to get through the night. Her headache hadn't gone away. It had simply shifted from the back to the front, which meant that on top of an overdose of tension, her sinuses were starting to act up.

And dammit, she was hungry! It was her own fault, which didn't make her feel one whit better. C. Cornelius had of-fered her supper. That is, if the dumping of a dozen or so cans in front of her could be construed as an invitation. She'd declined. In fact, once she'd gained the security of Hattie's bedroom, she'd refused to come out again.

Not that he'd insisted. Evidently, when the man had promised to leave her alone, he'd meant it.

For a little while she dozed, her dreams a jumble of chase scenes on hair-raising mountain roads and trying to pack tons of clothes into a tiny toilet case only to have them fly out and scatter all over the edge of a parking lot full of rusty blue sedans. But she was wide awake again when a soft rap on her door sent her heart banging against her ribs.

"Are you awake?"

She didn't move a muscle. The chair she'd jammed un-der the doorknob wouldn't have kept out a determined housefly.

So he'd finally shown his true colors. Just when she'd been ready to accept him as one of Hattie's harmless, if ec-centric, friends, if not actually her nephew, he was trying to sneak into her room at—goodness, what time was it?

Squinting at the luminous dial of her old high-school graduation watch, Marty discovered that it was barely ten o'clock. It felt like the middle of the night, but then she'd been up here for hours.

What now? What could he want this time of night? He'd promised to leave her alone, and she had definitely planned to return the favor. So maybe she'd panicked and acted a bit silly. And yes, she might even have glanced once or twice at his—ah, masculine assets. That still didn't give him any right to—

And anyway, his back had been to her. He couldn't have known what she was looking at.

Hearing his retreating footsteps on the stairway, she filled her lungs with slightly musty air. Whew! That had been a narrow escape. It was her own fault for getting herself into this position, but quite honestly, she hadn't known what else to do. She'd had the devil's own time finding someone who even knew where Hattie Davenport lived, much less someone willing to drive her all the way up. And the thought of walking out to the main road, if one could glorify a narrow, twisting cow path with such a term, had been too much to contemplate.

Martha waited for an hour to pass. And then another one. She was wide awake. Her headache had settled down to a monotonous throb, but her stomach was rumbling like a coal car.

A quarter to twelve. The witching hour. Better a witch, or even an ax murderer, than slow starvation. To function halfway decently, the female body—at least this particular model—required three squares a day, plus frequent doses of peanut-buttered Oreos. Plus, in times of stress or pollen, as many aspirins as the law allowed. Martyrdom had never held much appeal for her.

Nor had freezing to death, Martha conceded quickly as she eased one bare foot from under the covers. The minuscule fire had long since gone out, leaving the room icy and dank. Either the house wasn't insulated or the incredible bearded hulk didn't know diddly about fire building.

Her bathrobe, if she remembered correctly, was on the bottom of a ton of neatly folded clothes, wrapped around her precious collection of family photos. If she unpacked, she'd just have to repack, and it was hardly worth the effort, especially as she might have to make a fast getaway.

Besides, how long could it take to sneak down to that shelf full of pill bottles she'd seen in the downstairs bathroom, snitch a couple of aspirin and then circle by the kitchen for a jar of peanut butter and a spoon? Hot, sweet, milky tea would be great, but there was no point in pushing her luck.

Her eyes strayed to the large vertical portrait of a young man in unfaded jeans and a white shirt, his dark hair flopping over one deep-set, brooding eye. "What about it?" After all these years, she couldn't remember what Hattie had called him. Something short that had reminded her of an old Red Skelton character. Corny, short for Cornelius? Hardly! She'd definitely have remembered that.

Cautiously, Martha moved the chair, opened the door and checked for any sign of life. No lights, no sounds—nothing. Either upstairs or down. Moving silently across the bare hardwood floors, she glided down the stairs, using the banister for guidance, then wondered how on earth she was going to find her way through a dark, unfamiliar house that was booby-trapped with easels full of paintings and sculpture stands full of bronze busts, clay heads and marble thingamabobs. Not to mention a wild assortment of furniture that ranged from moth-eaten antique to classic art deco to city-dump chic.

She'd hand her that—Hattie had always had the courage of her convictions. One of the things that had drawn Martha to the eccentric artist all those years ago had been the fact that the two of them were so completely different. As a teenager and the motherless daughter of a small-time Yadkin County farmer, Martha had accepted her lot in life. Hattie, at whatever age she'd been then—one could never be quite sure—had accepted nothing. Her philosophy, which she'd shared at the drop of a hat, had been that if you didn't care for the hand you'd been dealt, you could toss it on the table and draw again. Life was a game, and most of the cards were wild.

Perhaps it had worked for Hattie. For Martha, it simply hadn't. For Martha, all the cards had been wild and she couldn't even find the game, much less try to play it.

"Ouch! Hellfire and tornadoes!" She hopped on one cold foot and nursed a toe of the other. What idiot would plant a chair right where people were supposed to walk?

If she hadn't been such a wimp, she'd have grabbed one of those cans C. Cornelius had tossed at her, then she wouldn't be creeping around in the dead of night in a booby-trapped house with an ax wielder probably breathing down her neck.

Dammit, she wasn't even dressed for the part! Weren't heroines supposed to wear something virginal and wispy? Wasn't a hero in a white hat supposed to swoop up in the nick of time and save her and her emerald from fire-breathing Odwells?

"What kind of heroine wears a yellow cotton nightgown from J. C. Penney?" she grumbled. "On sale, yet!"

Clement crawled forward, lowered his right knee onto a sharp rock and swore. If he ever found the blasted things, he was going to staple them to his temples. After that he was going to call his office and have Malvern mail his other pair. If he could get through on the blasted phone, that was.

And if he survived the night. In lieu of a robe, he'd worn an old lab coat over his pajamas. The first thing he'd learned was that lab coats were not designed for crawling. He'd left it by the wayside. The next thing he'd discovered was that pajama tops were just as much of a handicap to a man on his knees. The third time he'd crawled into his shirttail and practically strangled himself, he'd shed that, too. So now he was freezing to death, lacerating his hands and knees, and for all he knew, his damned glasses might be anywhere within a radius of fifty feet.

He'd located the chopping block by feel, then ventured out from there. It was slow going; and not just because of the darkness. He wouldn't have made much more headway in broad daylight. As it was, he used the flashlight as a dowsing rod, hoping to hear the clink of glass against metal.

His fingers encountered a jagged splinter and he swore. Somehow he'd managed to collect splinters on parts of his anatomy that had barely even seen the light of day. Not to mention the cuts, bruises and abrasions. Once he found the things, he'd probably have to fill Hattie's bathtub with an antibacterial solution and soak for a week.

If it hadn't been for the headache that always resulted from going without his glasses, he would have waited until morning to start searching, but he couldn't sleep with a headache and he was afraid to risk fumbling blind among Hattie's pill bottles for a remedy. She never threw out anything. The last time he'd looked for a simple antiseptic he'd had to paw through everything from outdated estrogen to something called Porter's Healing Oil.

Playing the flashlight across the ground at a low angle, Clement squinted into a darkness made even more mysterious by myopia and astigmatism, hoping to catch a glint of reflection from his lenses. It was hopeless. He'd have better luck trying to find a needle in a haystack. At least he could have used a magnet and been reasonably sure of eventual success.

He uttered a four-letter word that would have stunned his peers. It was one he'd never before had the courage to use, and he discovered that, as a relief valve, it was surprisingly effective.

However, it did little to solve his immediate problem.

Sighing, he clicked off the flashlight and tilted his head back, staring at a soft glow he assumed must be a cloud-covered moon. He couldn't even see the damned moon! He despised this feeling of helplessness, always had. He'd felt it too many times in his life, and no matter how he insulated himself with degrees, accomplishments and accolades, it had never ceased to bother him.

After a while he'd learned to curb his vulnerability by keeping to the relatively safe limits of laboratories, libraries and home.

If it weren't for Hattie, he'd probably have turned into a real recluse by now. She was the one who insisted on his getting out into what she called the real world now and then, and because he cared for her deeply, he made the effort.

But he hated it. He was always eager to get back into his comfortable shell. What was it they called those decapod crustaceans that took refuge in the cast-off shells of various univalve mollusks? Hermit crabs. Yes, he could empathize with those homely little fellows. All those long legs tripping over one another...

All of which was doing nothing to solve his immediate problem. He'd barely got to his feet when, without warning, the follicles on his scalp contracted. Blinking owlishly in the darkness, he swung around, tripped on a chunk of split oak and landed on his backside.

"Aha!"

The triumphant cry came from somewhere near the garage. Twisting to one side, Clement palpated his bruised gluteous maximus. Before he could determine the extent of his latest injury, he sneezed.

"I don't know how you found me, you rotten little creep, but I'm warning you—if you don't get out of here this minute, I'm going to wake everyone in the house, and you'll be sorry you ever even *thought* about stealing my emerald!"

It was his paranoid houseguest. He sneezed again.

"You can't fool me, Hubert Odwell. I know who you are, and—and so does the sheriff! I gave him your license number, and that phony business card of yours, so if I were you, I'd get a move on. People around here don't take kindly to crumby jerks who prey on women and try to steal from them."

"Martha—"

"Hush! Don't even try to talk me into anything. I don't want to hear a word out of you, and by the way—it might interest you to know that I'm armed. You have thirty seconds to get in your car and get out of here, because if I lose my temper, I'll *use* this thing!"

"I can't drive. I told you that."

"You can't dri—C. Cornelius? Is that *you*?" Her voice dwindled off like a stuck balloon. "Oh, glory," she murmured.

"I didn't mean to frighten you."

"What are you doing out here? Stargazing?"

"Glasses. Feeling for them. I don't want to mistake estrogen for acetaminophen."

"No, no, of course you don't," Martha murmured soothingly.

Irritated, he wondered if she thought he was going to resort to violence over a pair of lost spectacles. Dammit, he'd told her precisely what he was doing and why. It was only in a social situation that he found it difficult to articulate co-herently. "This isn't social," he argued. "You do under-stand that, don't you?"

"Oh, yes. Yes, I do, I understand perfectly." She was backing away. He could hear the sounds quite clearly.

Bending over, Clem felt for the flashlight, which he'd dropped when she'd startled him. It had evidently rolled away. "Although relatively speaking, I suppose it is," he murmured, wanting to keep her there. Even though she was somewhat strange, he found himself drawn to her for rea-sons that escaped him completely. Normally, he'd have hid out in the woods all night to escape such an encounter.

"Is what?" she asked warily. At least she'd stopped re-treating.

"Social." He moved forward, hands held out in front of him like a shield. "That is, depending on one's—"

"Stay back! Stay right where you are. Social or not, that's far enough!"

He could see her now. At least he could see a faint pale column against the inky shadow of a yew tree. He wasn't nearly close enough. Clem found himself wanting to touch her again, to smell that faint fragrance he'd detected ear-lier. He wanted to know who she was and what she was doing there and where she'd come from and what she thought about—about everything. He wanted to *talk* to her, wonder of wonders! That in itself was a problem. How was it possible for a man to spend his entire life in pursuit of knowledge and not learn the basic art of communicating with another human being on a personal level?

Hell, even the birds and bees managed *that* much!

"Would you please read labels for me?" he blurted. If he could get her to do that much, it would be a beginning. Quite aside from the fact that he needed her eyes, he rather desperately needed to keep her around long enough to ex-

amine and evaluate his startling physical reaction to the
sound of her voice and the scent that seemed to surround
her. It had never happened to him before—at least not in a
long, long time.

"Labels? You mean like *food*?" she asked, and he detected a slight lessening of wariness.

"Medication first. On the shelf. Going without glasses
gives me a headache. Without them, I can't read the labels."

And then she was beside him. Taking his arm, she urged
him toward the house, and Clem let his hand slip down and
clasp hers as they moved cautiously through the dark yard.
"Watch that branch," she warned, her voice husky against
the crisp night air. "For pity's sake, C. Cornelius, why
didn't you say so in the first place? And you can't even see
to find them, either, can you? But why on earth did you wait
until the middle of the night?"

As Clement could no longer recall the line of reasoning
that had led him to sit in the darkened study for hours after
she'd locked herself into the bedroom upstairs, he didn't
bother even to attempt a reply.

She led him to the house as if he were a small child and
she were his nanny—although come to think of it, his nanny
had used a harness on him until he'd refused to wear it.
From then on, he'd heeled at command rather than have her
drag him along.

Two hands, palm to palm. It was a strange sensation.
Clement couldn't decide if he liked it or not. The trouble
was, he seemed to be losing control of the situation.

"If you'll share your headache remedy with me, I'll read
you all the labels you want, but you really should have a
spare pair of glasses. Or contacts."

"Yes."

"Back to monosyllables." She opened the door and guided him over the sill. Clement could have told her that he was fine on familiar territory. Like any sight-impaired person, he'd made a point of familiarizing himself with the house in case of such an event.

"Come sit down over here and tell me where to find the aspirin." Leaving the rolling pin on the table, she led him to a hideous purple plush chair and he let himself be led, not sure whether he was enjoying the attention or frustrated by it.

Frustrated by something, that was becoming increasingly clear. Maybe she was right to be wary around him. "Acetylsalicylate or acetaminophen. Not the ibuprofen—that's for Hattie's hands."

He missed her presence for the few moments she was gone, and the fact intrigued him. It was totally foreign to his nature, for he was the quintessential loner. Impatiently he waited for her to reappear. He didn't even know what she looked like—not really. He knew only the sound of her voice—he liked it very much. And the way she smelled. He definitely liked that!

"You're back," he said, and felt an immediate rush of embarrassment at so gauche an observation.

"I'll get us some water. Or milk, if you have it. I skipped too many meals today. Normally I eat like a horse, but what with one thing and another..."

"There's milk. There's food, too."

She laughed, and every sensory organ in his body registered the effect. "So you keep trying to tell me, but so far, I haven't got closer than the outside of a can."

"Martha Eberly," Clement repeated after he'd taken two of the capsules and downed a glass of icy well water. "Will you talk to me?"

"Talk to you? About what?" Martha set her glass carefully on an enameled table.

Clement tried to think of something fascinating to say. What did men talk about with women? Women who weren't scientists? "You're *not* a scientist, are you?" he asked, although he was fairly certain of the answer.

"A scientist? Goodness, no! I'm not anything—at least not yet."

There didn't seem to be a lot he could say to that. She'd effectively shut off any discussion of work. He couldn't very well ask her about her work if she didn't have any, nor could he discuss his own. It would turn into a monologue, and a technical one at that, and then she would either walk away or say something cutting, and this time, he didn't want it to end that way.

He'd once invited a woman to a movie and they'd gone for three hours without exchanging a single word. A month later he'd worked up his nerve and asked her out to dinner and she'd said no thanks, she'd rather spend a lively evening alone watching dust settle on her furniture. It had been a year before he'd tried again. The next time he'd chosen a woman who had talked nonstop about football players and clothes, and he hadn't bothered to ask her out again. Not that she would have gone.

Martha sighed.

Clement sighed. If only he could have seen her, he might have gauged the situation more accurately. However, she was still here. She hadn't walked away yet, and that was a favorable sign, wasn't it?

Taking courage from that small fact, he said cheerfully, "Well. What would you like to talk about?"

"What would I— How about food?"

"All right." Food? What was there to say about it? He'd much rather know about the man who'd frightened her and why she was here and where she'd come from and where she was—

"We're going to *talk* about it? Is that *all*?" she exclaimed.

She sounded exasperated, and for the life of him Clem didn't know why. He'd thought things were progressing unusually well. Here they were, seated across the table from one another, having shared a companionable dose of acetaminophen, yet she seemed—tense.

"Uh—all? No. You go first—what do you find interesting about food?"

Hmm... Not bad for a beginner, he thought a little smugly. Conversation wasn't all that difficult once you got the hang of it—make a statement and then follow up with a question. That way, there was a reciprocal interchange of ideas instead of the dead end at which he so often found himself stranded.

He could tell she had leaned forward. The pale blur shifted. "The lack of it, at the moment," she snapped. "It's all I can think about."

Evidently she didn't know the rules of conversation. First a statement, then a question. What was he supposed to say now?

He cleared his throat, then he sneezed.

"Bless you," she muttered. "Do you have a cold?"

He beamed. They were off again!

"Why, thank you. That's very kind of you. No." *Now, ask her something, wonderboy!* Like what makes her smell the way she does. Like why the touch of her hand on his arm should cause a physiological reaction in practically every system in his body, with the possible exception of the digestive system.

Intellectually he knew the answer, yet for some reason the data kept falling apart in his mind when he attempted to analyze it.

"As I was saying," Martha went on a bit grimly, "I never sleep too well on an empty stomach."

"Physiologically, the favored position is supine, not prone. That is, you should sleep on your back, or at least on your side. You see, the cervical vertebrae—"

"Stuff your cervical vertebrae! I'm hungry, dammit!"

Clement blinked at the outburst. Had he offended her? His usual offense was boring his partner, but she didn't sound bored. She sounded... "Hungry?"

"Famished."

He groaned. Of course she was. That's what she'd meant when she'd mentioned missing meals. Myopic and astigmatic eyes glinted blue with flecks of gold as Clement rose and held out a hand. "I, too. Hungry, that is. You choose, I'll open."

"I thought you'd never ask." She got to her feet and peered toward the kitchen with a look of anticipation. "Better yet, how about I cook, we both eat. You do have eggs, don't you?"

"Yes."

"Bacon?"

"No."

"Oh, well... Bread?"

"Frozen."

"It'll thaw. I'm a great hand at thawing. How about cheese?"

"Yes. Interesting mold patterns. A type of penicillin, you know."

Martha halted in the door of the kitchen. "Mold? Um— what kind of cheese is it?"

"The label says Rocquefort."

Her hesitation was barely noticeable. "Scrambled eggs with Rocquefort it is. Sounds heavenly."

But Clement, hungry though he was, was momentarily distracted by the clean, feminine scent that eddied around her. She was yellow from the floor up, but still pale copper on top. Her arms and her face were pink, as if she'd recently been exposed to an excessive amount of ultraviolet radiation.

"Look, you're going to have to tell me where things are. How's your headache, by the way?" She brushed past him and he heard the whisper of fabric on flesh. He swallowed hard, rooted to the spot and tingling with a variety of sensations he'd have given his eyeteeth to explore. "Um—what are you wearing, Martha?"

"I'm glad you asked that question." She placed several things on the counter and shut the door. "My nightgown."

"You are?" He beamed, feeling as if he'd just been knighted. "It was a good question then?" He could visualize her smiling, hear the sound of it in her voice, and it pleased him inordinately. Really, they were getting along superbly! She was obviously a very perceptive woman.

"I'm glad you asked because if you'd been able to see what I was wearing, I wouldn't be wearing it. What I mean is, I wouldn't be here. Like this, I mean. Good Lord, I'm beginning to sound like you."

"You are? Is that good?"

She shoved a bowl in his hands and said, "Beat these. Gently, now—don't slosh. Will coffee keep you awake, or would you prefer hot milk?"

"I want to stay awake. I could talk all night, couldn't you?" He felt something cold and wet land on the top of his foot. The bowl was abruptly removed from his hands, and he could hear her stirring gently with a whisk. Maybe he'd been a bit too enthusiastic. He hoped he hadn't made too big a mess of it.

She handed him a paper towel, and he wiped the egg off his foot, hoping he hadn't spilled it on his pajamas, as well. Damn—he'd left his shirt outside. He would never have risked offending her again by appearing half naked if he'd been thinking straight.

"No, C. Cornelius, I couldn't talk all night," she said, sounding distinctly unoffended. She was a kind person, he decided. "As tired as I am, I'm even hungrier than that. So let's have our supper and get to bed, because tomorrow I need to get an early start if I'm going to find a ride to Asheville in time to catch the bus home."

Four

Clement was determined to keep her there. He didn't know how, much less why. All he knew was that it was vitally important that she stay long enough to—

Long enough for him to...

Swearing softly, he shoved both hands through his hair, raking it from his brow. It occurred to him that he'd needed a haircut when he'd left Winston. By now there was no telling what he looked like. No wonder she'd been wary of him.

Martha. Who was she? Intellectual curiosity had driven him since he'd barely been able to walk, only this was something entirely different. After a few hours in her presence, he was possessed by a compelling urge to explore every facet of her mind and body.

It wasn't going to work. In fact, it was scary as hell! Trying to relate to a woman who didn't really interest him turned him into a tongue-tied jerk. What would happen with a woman who mattered to him?

Clem wanted badly to think he'd made real progress tonight, but ruthless self-honesty was too ingrained. He'd
managed to get through an hour without making an abso-
lute ass of himself.

On the other hand, for him, even that much was a
considerable accomplishment.

He paced in a well-worn pattern. He'd always paced when
faced with a conundrum, and this one had him stumped.
Why Martha Eberly? Why some woman whose voice he'd
heard a few times, whose face he had yet to see clearly? Why
not the lovely young biochemist who'd come to work for
B.F.I. last fall? He'd spent three months working up enough
nerve to ask her out to dinner, then been so relieved when
she'd turned him down that he'd gone home and drunk
himself into a stupor—a matter of three beers.

Martha. The name suited her. There was a gentle quality
about the name and about the woman. He didn't know how
he knew, but he'd felt it right from the first. Strength and
vulnerability—fear and daring. And compassion. Look at
the way she'd taken him on in the backyard, after seeing the
flashlight and thinking an intruder was snooping around,
about to break into Hattie's house.

And the way she'd taken his hand and led him inside.

She was warm and soft, and she smelled like fresh baked
bread and roses, with a hint of something more intimate that
stirred him in a way he hadn't been stirred in a long time.

Clem told himself sternly that it was purely a matter of
hormones. It had to be. But regardless of the cause, it was
a definite fact, which was unfortunate, as he didn't have a
snowball's chance in hell of alleviating the attendant dis-
comfort. He'd always had excellent control over both his
mind and his body, but something told him that control of
his was going to be severely challenged before Martha
Eberly turned tail and headed down the mountain.

Clement tugged at his beard. If he'd been slated to have that sort of relationship with a woman, it would have occurred before now. He was thirty-two years old. All the longing and all the luck in the world couldn't alter the fact that he hadn't the least idea of how to ask a woman to lie down and let him—

That is, to take off her clothes and allow—

Well, dammit, what did a man *do*? How did he go about setting the scene? And if, wonder of wonders, the woman proved willing, what then? Who undressed first? Was it a mutual or a reciprocal arrangement? Besides, how did he know he could—that is, that *it* would—

Oh, the devil! His head was pounding again, and he hadn't a chance of getting to sleep in this frame of mind.

It was inevitable, perhaps, that Clem's mind would home in on the single most painful memory in a voluminous and orderly mental file. A memory that should have been discarded years ago.

He'd been in grad school at the time—about fifteen and incredibly naive. Due to his age, he'd been put in a freshman dorm. If the term "wimp" had been popular at the time, it would've been used to describe him, but there'd been others, equally descriptive, and he'd been called them all.

How many times had he wished he'd been born with the I.Q. of a chimp? Or better yet, a tortoise. Bright enough to manage survival and procreation; incapable of worrying about much else. By now he might even have been married to Georgina Duffy.

Black hair, blue eyes, with a pouting mouth and a body that had temporarily nullified roughly a hundred thousand dollars worth of education from his mind the first time he'd ever laid eyes on her, Georgina had been a waitress at the student union. Clement had cut classes, meals and everything else just to watch her move around the room. The first time she'd smiled at him, he'd gone catatonic.

His condition, of course, had been pathetically obvious to his roommates, Rolf and Bucky, both of whom had been in their early twenties. Always the butt of jokes, he'd suddenly become the chief source of entertainment on his hall, and with his usual denseness, he'd quite misunderstood. Like a fool, he'd smiled and lapped up the unaccustomed attention.

It had been a cinch for them to talk him into attending the post-game party at the home of one of the students. All they'd had to do was to tell him Georgina would be there. If they'd spread it on too thick, told him she was panting to get to know him better, Clement wouldn't have gone within a mile of the place. He'd been quite content to worship quietly from a safe distance. It was all he'd known how to do.

But they'd played it just right. Rolf had given him a pep talk and Bucky had talked him out of wearing his beige suit, pin-striped shirt and knit tie. Together they'd fixed him up with a pair of faded jeans that were long enough and a Hawaiian print shirt.

Once there, they'd settled him in a quiet corner where he could watch the goings-on without getting in the way and offered to bring him a drink.

"Fruit punch? You gotta be kidding," Rolf had said. "Hell, man, we got to celebrate! I'll bring you a beer, right? Forty-six to zip, man! Did we stomp their tight ends into the mud, or what?"

Clement, who was far more familiar with tithonometers than he was with tight ends, had maintained some vestige of self-preservation. "I'd better stick with the punch. I'm still underage, you know," he'd said, blossoming under the rare camaraderie.

That was the night he'd learned about vodka. That was the night he'd learned about a lot of things. By the time Georgina had migrated over to his corner, he was leaning against the wall, grinning foolishly. The grin didn't waver when she stopped in front of him, although when she leaned forward and breathed on his lenses, fogging them up, his knees had threatened to buckle.

"Come on, honey, you need to get out of this hot ol' place and breathe a little cool air."

He didn't remember going with her. Nor had he been aware of all the snickers, the swift glances. Looking back, he was surprised he'd been able to navigate on his own. Or perhaps he'd had some help. What he did remember was a dimly lighted library with a leather sofa that had felt shockingly cold to the touch. He remembered Georgina's fingers on his chest—she'd been saying something about loosening his buttons and his belt so that he could breathe. He remembered more or less collapsing so that his cheek was pillowed on her chest, which was even softer than it looked. Her perfume had been strong and cloying, and he remembered turning so that his nose would clear the swell of her right breast.

The next thing he remembered was waking up to see a ring of faces, male and female, all around him. Georgina had been trying to talk over all the laughter, but she'd been giggling too hard. "Oh, come on, guys, haven't I earned a beer? Leave the poor baby alone."

There'd been an immediate outcry, and she'd waved it down. "All right, all right, so what d'you want, a demo or a blow-by-blow description?"

Clement had prayed to die. It was either that or disgrace himself even further by throwing up on his borrowed shirt.

"Hey, take it from me, guys, it takes more than brains to—"

There'd been a chorus of irreverent comments, and someone had shouted, "Come on, Georgie, what's his I.Q.?"

"A lot bigger than yours, Bucky boy," she'd retorted, and there'd been another roar of laughter, and some squeals from the female members of the group.

It had been then that Clement had realized that except for his shoes, socks and the lurid shirt, which barely managed to preserve his modesty, he was stark naked. Just as another roar of laughter broke over him he'd felt the first wave of nausea.

"Okay, okay, you've had your fun—I know I have," she'd purred, and Clement hadn't waited to hear any more. He'd leaped off the sofa and windmilled his way through the crowd, uncaring of his near-nude state. He'd been sick as a dog, and it was only because he hadn't been able to lift his head off the pillow the next morning that he hadn't left school, the country and possibly the universe.

He'd like to think that he'd proved something by staying on after the most humiliating experience of his life. But in the end, all he'd proved was that he couldn't tolerate alcohol and he was a dead loss where women were concerned. Either he didn't have what it took to please them or he didn't know how. The result was the same. Since then, he'd never risked another disaster.

The positive result had been that he'd been able to throw himself wholeheartedly into his studies at a time when most boys his age had been distracted by more exciting pursuits.

Martha lay awake until the eastern sky began to turn gray. Hattie's soft mattress was a swaybacked nightmare for someone used to flat and hard. Every bone and muscle in her body ached. She hadn't been able to get comfortable enough to sleep, and the more she lay awake, the more she worried.

Worry had always come easy to Martha, starting from the time when her mother had been diagnosed as terminally ill. Later she'd worried about her father, who had relied on her mother far more than any man should have done. She'd worried about her brother, Jack, who'd hated farming and joined the army with a view to earning himself a college education.

Finally, after Jack had been educated and married, with a family of his own in Kentucky, and her father had sold his tobacco allotment, got rid of all the stock except for a cow, a few laying hens and three coon dogs and retired to the front porch rocker to wait for his heart to stop ticking, she'd worried about her own future.

And felt selfish and unworthy for doing so.

Rubbing gritty-feeling eyes, she sat up in bed, taking perverse pleasure in the bite of cold air through her thin cotton gown. She had truly done all she could have done...hadn't she? After Papa had died and the farm had been sold, there'd been enough money to get her started in school, although she'd already been having second thoughts about majoring in art. By that time, Hattie had retired and moved away, and with her inspiration reduced to the occasional letter, Martha had just about decided on a business major when Jack's wife had gone into early labor and died giving birth to a daughter. Martha had dropped everything to go take care of her two-and-a-half-year-old nephew and her newborn niece.

And despite the tragic circumstances, she'd loved it. She'd done a pretty good job, too, considering she'd never been around children all that much. But growing up on a farm, with both parents ailing in their last years, she'd learned about care giving. In the midst of juggling meals and laundry and a thousand other tasks, she'd often been frustrated, often impatient with her own shortcomings. But in retrospect, it had been deeply satisfying. So much so that she'd all but decided, now that Jack was remarried and she was no longer needed, to go into nurse's training.

And then she'd found that blasted emerald, and having found the thing, she refused to allow some crook to steal it from her. She had about four hundred dollars left from her part of the sale of the farm—Jack had needed a down payment on a house, and she'd gladly lent it to him, but she still had her training to pay for. Four hundred dollars wasn't nearly enough, and she'd lain awake nights wondering where she was going to get the rest, because with a new wife and two children, it would be years before Jack's paycheck would stretch to loan payments.

Worrying? Martha was an expert at worrying. Which was obviously something C. Cornelius didn't believe in. Up here all alone, blind as a bat, unable to drive or even to communicate effectively, it was a wonder he'd survived! Not that he looked all that helpless. He didn't look helpless at all, in fact. But it was pretty clear that the man needed a keeper.

Unbidden, a vision of his tall, beautifully constructed body took shape in her mind. Her breath quickened. What on earth was she thinking of? He'd wrapped an ax around her backside and scared the wits out of her! He was wild, bushy-headed, totally unpredictable, and if her brain hadn't slipped into neutral, she'd have been out of here so fast!

All right, to be ruthlessly honest, which she always tried to be and occasionally succeeded, Martha knew that it hadn't been paralysis that had kept her from running away when he'd let her go.

There'd been something about him...something sort of...

Which was ridiculous! No woman with a grain of common sense would admit to being attracted to someone like

C. Cornelius. Because even if he did turn out to be Hattie's nephew, he must be some sort of black sheep. She'd only ever heard of one nephew, the one in the portrait. The brainy one. And if C. Cornelius even *had* a brain, he managed to keep it pretty well hidden.

On the other hand, he was sort of sweet. And his rear end was worthy of attention by even the most seasoned man watcher. Which she wasn't.

Martha's gaze strayed to the portrait on the opposite wall. She could recall the first time she'd ever seen it in Hattie's west end house in Winston. She'd been smitten and painfully transparent, no doubt, because Hattie had answered her unasked questions, telling her that the subject had been something of a prodigy.

At the time, Martha hadn't even been sure what a prodigy was, but she'd been deeply impressed by the sensitive face, the long jaw and the deep set, brooding eyes.

What had Hattie called him? Lordy, it had been so long ago! She'd fallen in and out of love with any number of movie and TV stars since then. And Virgil, of course.

It had been something distinctly ungeniuslike. Hank? Clyde? Clem! That was it—Clem. Martha remembered being disappointed at his name. She'd rechristened him Ian in her mind—or had it been Sean? And then Hattie had moved away, and she'd forgotten all about him until she'd seen the portrait again.

It was gradually growing light outside. Pale yellow warmed the gray, pushing back the darkness. Mist hugged the ground, blackening the tree trunks, and reluctantly Martha eased herself out of bed and hurried into the cold bathroom. There was an electric strip heater, but it was no match for the high-ceilinged room. There was also a radiator, which, like the one in her bedroom, was barely lukewarm.

Speed and a tub of hot water would have to serve. And serve quickly if she intended to walk to the nearest town, check on buses and hire someone to come haul her luggage in to town.

After turning on the hot-water faucet full blast, she dashed into the bedroom and was digging a set of clean clothes out of her suitcase when she heard the bellowing sound from downstairs. Clutching a set of underwear and a pair of white socks, she went to the door, opened it a crack and listened.

"C. Cornelius? Was that you?" she called hesitantly. And then, when there was no reply, she yelled louder. "Cornelius! Are you all right?"

"No!"

Oh, Lord, what had he done now? Praying that he hadn't retrieved his glasses since she'd last seen him, she hurried downstairs, following the sound of his angry voice.

"Damned antiquated system," Clement grumbled as he slapped the walls in search of a towel, which he finally located by tripping on it. He muttered something profane about modern plumbing, touched briefly on the Greeks and the Romans and jammed his toe against the edge of the door. It was bad enough that the second bathroom upstairs hadn't worked in years. It was even worse that any time two people attempted to use the remaining two at the same time, one of them risked either frostbite or scalding. Hattie had explained the vagaries of the plumbing system to him, and during the week she'd spent getting him acclimated before she'd left for New York and ultimately Greece, they'd worked out a schedule for bath taking.

"Cornelius! Where are you?"

Not content merely to freeze him to death, she had now come to gloat! Unthinking, Clement threw open the bath-oom door and glared at the pale shape hovering in the dark allway. "It was *my* turn!" he announced indignantly.

"Oh, my Lord," whispered the shape.

Either she was praying or she was in shock. That particular tone of voice was difficult to interpret. As random atches of soap suds slowly slid down his chest and his right igh, Clem continued to squint at her.

And then it suddenly struck him that just because he ouldn't see her, that didn't mean she was similarly handiapped. With a strangled sound, he slammed the door between them and leaned against it, breathing raggedly. Was e out of his moth-eaten mind? He'd lived alone for so long e could no longer even be trusted among civilized people!

Several minutes later, chastely saronged with a monorammed mauve-on-purple towel, Clement opened the door crack and peered out. The fear of seeing a ring of grining faces was subliminal, but very real nevertheless.

"Martha?" he whispered experimentally.

No response.

Thank God! If he'd actually thought there was the lightest possibility that she was still lurking in the shadws, he would have barricaded himself in the bathroom for he next six weeks.

Where the hell was his bathrobe? Or rather, the lab coat hat substituted for a robe?

In the backyard, of course, along with his pajama top and is damned glasses. Which, by now, were probably broken r trampled into the ground.

Clem hadn't thought to bring a change of clothes with im when he'd hurried down for his regular early morning hower. Having had the run of the house, he'd tended to fall nto a few bad habits, at least one of which he was going to ave to shed immediately.

And dammit, the minute Hattie got back into the country he was going to prevail on her to drive him into town
where he could get himself a decent bathrobe! And a few
new shirts in a larger size. And—well, hell, why not? A pair
of blue jeans. The pale, streaky kind with the label on the
rear end.

Clement headed for the back stairs, praying he wouldn't
be discovered. His beard dripped on his chest, and a drop
of cold water wove its way through the thicket there and
headed south. The towel felt clammy on his backside. It
barely covered him. There wasn't a real man-size towel in the
entire house, and he wasn't built for tea towels.

He'd thought he'd made some real progress last night, but
he'd really blown it with this stunt. He should've kept his
mouth shut and gone ahead with his cold shower, even
though the immediate need had passed. She couldn't know
that when anyone turned on the hot water upstairs, it instantly shut it off all over the rest of the system.

And if she was still here by the time he got dressed, he'd
probably need another ice-cold dousing. Maybe it was for
the best, he told himself, knowing full well that he was way
beyond any pretense at intellectual honesty.

By the time Clement worked up his nerve to go downstairs again, fully dressed this time, he had put his embarrassment behind him. He'd had a lifetime of experience in
putting embarrassing episodes behind him. Embarrassment was merely a state of mind, accompanied by certain
characteristic physiological changes—most of which he'd
learned to control before he'd reached voting age.

"Well," he said calmly to the unfamiliar yellow blur at
the head of the table.

"There's coffee made, and I can scramble you another
egg. There are more in the carton."

"I do eggs quite well." He refused to have her think of him as helpless, along with everything else. All right, so maybe he hadn't managed to extinguish quite all of his embarrassment.

"Without your glasses?"

"It's a simple matter of putting them in a pan, running water over them and increasing the temperature until the protoplasm is sufficiently coagulated. It's all in the timing—allowing, of course, for the altitude." Which should show her that he was in no danger of starving if she walked out.

But in spite of what he'd told himself, Clem knew that he wasn't about to allow her to leave. For reasons he didn't dare go into, it had become vitally important to him that she stay on. At least until he'd proved that he wasn't a complete ass.

He could hear her stirring her coffee, and the aroma of it made his nose twitch. He walked directly to the cabinet that held the cups, took down a large one and set it on the table. Right on top of the cup and saucer she'd already laid out for him. Something broke.

"Sit *down*!" Martha barked. It was a soft bark, but it didn't lack authority for all that. "You stay put until I get back, you hear me?"

Clement sat. Had he thought he could control his emotions? He was in worse shape than he'd been seventeen years ago, when he'd slept through his own debauchment and awakened to discover himself surrounded by an appreciative audience. He had a subliminal vision of waking up one morning to see Martha standing over him, laughing her head off because he'd tried to make love to her and failed miserably.

Oh, hell, he had to get out of there. He would walk, run, climb—anything, as long as it took him away from thi woman!

Jumping up, he felt a sharp pain in his right heel and heard something grate on the floor. Before he could react to either, the door opened and she was back. Clement dropped into the chair, resigned to his ignominious fate.

"They were right where you left them," Martha announced. "Muddy, though—no wonder you couldn't find them. I'll just rinse them off. It must have rained in the night."

"I didn't leave them, I knocked them off and then couldn't see to find them," he muttered sullenly.

"Whatever. Here you are, Cinderella—a perfect fit." She slid the pair of plastic-rimmed spectacles on his nose and hooked the wings over his ears, and Clem remembered chagrined, that he'd been intending to get new frames for several years. These had been mended in three places with adhesive tape. Tape that was now grimy and frayed.

Martha laid a hand on his shoulder. If he'd been hooked up to a voltmeter, the needle would have jammed. "You ought to get a hanger for them next time you go to town. Who's going to find them for you after I leave?"

"You're not leaving." So much for subtlety.

She snatched back her hand, and Clement settled the glasses properly on his nose and turned an apologetic look on her. "Not yet? Please?" He couldn't let her go until he made sure he could find her again. If she would allow him to escort her wherever she was headed, then he'd have an address—something. Or even time enough on the way to convince her to stay with him.

Why hadn't he stuck with driving until he'd mastered it? Any idiot could drive. Statistics proved it. It would have been the perfect solution. He could practically hear himself saying nonchalantly, "Stick around for a few more days,

oney, and I'll drive you wherever you're going and help
ou get settled. You'll need someone to carry your bags for
ou."

"What?" Martha exploded. "You told me you didn't
rive, and I believed you! And all this time you were lying
o me, and here I've been—"

Oh, hell, he'd done it again. Spoken his thoughts aloud.
ome men weren't fit to be let out without a leash and a
uzzle. "No! I mean, I don't. Drive, that is—no car. Hat-
e's is—but I can't—if I owned a car, I'd give it to you.
lease believe me, Martha."

She slid into the chair across from him, and Clem stared
t her raptly, seeing her clearly for the first time. She was
uite simply the most beautiful creature he had ever beheld
 his long and uneventful life.

"Stop staring, you're making me self-conscious. How can
 believe any man who says one thing one minute and an-
ther thing the next? And any man who'd offer to give his
ar to a stranger is wacko. C. Cornelius, if you expect a
erson to believe anything you say, try leveling off at a sen-
ible altitude and sticking to the simple truth for a change,
kay?"

"Yes," he said dutifully. "There's my name, to start
ith."

"C. Cornelius? I thought it was sort of pretentious. What
o your friends call you? C? Neil?"

"My—uh—associates call me Clement. Or Dr. Barto. Or
ir. But Hattie calls me Clem," he added with a hopeful
xpression that elicited a soft groan from the woman across
rom him. "If you don't like it, you can call me something
lse," he added quickly.

Martha hadn't missed the evasion. The man didn't have
ny friends—not real friends. At least, no one who came to
nind immediately. But worst of all—or best of all, she
vasn't sure which—he was Hattie's Clem. *Her* Clem of the

sensitive face and the vulnerable mouth and the deep brooding eyes, only now all that was hidden behind thick lenses and that gosh-awful beard. That hauntingly beautiful boy in a man's body.

And it was *definitely* a man's body, all right! Martha had seen all the evidence she needed to on that score. Those broad shoulders, the narrow hips and long legs—and that fascinating pattern of wiry black hair that collected most heavily in the one area where she hadn't dared to allow her eyes to linger.

She looked at him as searchingly as he was studying her and decided that never in her life had she met a lonelier, a loster, a more endearingly vulnerable man.

For the moment, it completely escaped her that she couldn't wait to get away from him. Besides, it was only common decency to stay long enough to be sure he could look after himself until Hattie got home. She owed her old friend *that* much, at least, for befriending a naive young girl fresh off a tobacco farm and teaching her about art, about people and about life outside Yadkin County.

Suddenly embarrassed to realize she'd been staring, she asked the first thing that popped into her head. "Why did you tell me your name was C. Cornelius?"

Clement shrugged. "I don't know."

"I think I do. You were hiding. It doesn't take a psychologist to know that you'd do almost anything to keep strangers from getting too close to you. Any man who's reluctant even to share his first name..."

"It sounds childish when you put it like that."

"Even the glasses. And that gosh-awful beard."

He lifted a hand to cover his chin. "You don't like beards?"

"I don't like them or dislike them," she dismissed, "but how do you ever hope to make friends when you won't even share your face with them?"

"I don't— It's, uh—grown since I got here. I, um—didn't bring a razor."

"Well, I did. And there's bound to be a pair of scissors around here somewhere."

"Samson."

"Beg pardon?"

"Hair."

"Are we back to monosyllables again? Look, I'm not threatening to cut off anything, I was only making an observation. If you're finished with your coffee, I'll wash up. Or did you want something more?"

Clem's stomach tightened in anticipation, and he quelled it with a silent command. He wasn't about to allow her to cook for him, not when she already thought he was a dead loss. One way or another, he was determined to repair his reputation before she got away, because he couldn't bear the thought of her remembering him as a clown who couldn't take three steps without tripping over his own feet.

If she remembered him at all.

"Which way is town from here? I thought I'd go find out if a bus does come through, and then see if I could hire someone to drive me back and pick up my bags."

Clement began to panic. "You don't mean town."

"I do mean town."

"Asheville's too far. There's Cat Creek."

"I thought this *was* Cat Creek."

"Post office."

"Bus stop? Good glory, I'm beginning to sound just like you!"

Clement stood up, his smile a well-kept secret under his overgrown beard. He had his vision back, and Asheville was too far to walk, and he was reasonably certain that no bus came within ten miles of Cat Creek township. With advantages like those, he could conquer the world!

Five

———

They'd gone less than a mile when Martha stopped suddenly. If it had happened three weeks ago, Clement would have plowed into her and sent them both tumbling down the steep grade, but almost a month of daily hiking and climbing, not to mention the fortresslike stack of wood he'd split, had done wonders for his coordination.

"Did you change your mind?" he asked. The trail was easy here, and he'd allowed her to push past him and lead the way. For now.

"I walked right off and forgot all about it. I can't believe I did that!" Eyes wide in her flushed face, she grabbed one of his arms and shook it. "Clement, don't you understand? Anyone could walk in off the road and steal it. You *did* lock up, didn't you?"

"Lock what?" Was she feeling all right? She looked all right. God, yes—she looked extremely all right!

"The doors. The windows. What does a person usually lock when he leaves a house to go out?"

"I don't know."

She gave his arm another shake. Actually, it was not at all an unpleasant sensation. In fact, he discovered that he rather liked being touched, in any way at all, by her. Clement smiled at her—she was quite strong for someone so small. Her head only came up to his pectoral region.

"What do you mean, you don't know? You don't remember whether or not you *locked up*?"

"I meant that I don't know what people usually lock up when they go out," Clement explained patiently. "I suppose it depends on what they value most. But my memory is adequate—quite good, in fact."

The sound that emerged from somewhere in the region of her throat was part groan, part scream. "For once, can you concentrate on a simple question long enough to give a simple answer? Did you or did you not lock the house before we left?"

"Yes, usually I concentrate quite well, and my answers are always direct. And yes, I did."

Abruptly, she let go of his arm and sat on a mossy slope, drawing her knees up. Clement watched as she lowered her head so that her chin rested on her crossed arms. He felt a strong need to touch her hair, to experience for himself the texture that could gleam with metallic brilliance yet look as soft as a vapor.

Instead, he cleared his throat and turned to stare across the ravine to the ragged blue skyline in the distance. He'd been talking quite freely, in complete, coherent sentences. And yet something was still missing. Try as he would, he couldn't seem to get the knack of conversing. The flow was lacking—the easy give-and-take that went on among the more junior members of his staff.

Choosing a place several feet away, he lowered himself to the ground and sat awkwardly, hands dangling from his widespread knees. "Who is Hubert Odwell, Martha?" He'd planned to wait until he'd gained her confidence before prying into her personal affairs, but he couldn't afford to wait any longer. She was frightened. Both evidence and instinct told him that Odwell was responsible for the way she overreacted. "At least tell me why he's following you."

She looked stricken. "How do you know someone's following me?"

"The phone calls."

"But I never mentioned his name—I know I didn't!" She was twisting her hands, and Clem reached out and covered them both with one of his.

"Last night," he said in what he hoped was a calming tone. "When you thought I was an intruder, you called me Hubert Odwell."

She sagged, but she didn't try to pull away. Gradually, the panic faded from her eyes, leaving only a tired sort of wariness that made him want to gather her into his arms and say something poetic and heroic.

Which would, of course, have the effect of making her laugh. Laughter was better than fear; unfortunately, he could think of nothing either heroic or poetic at the moment. "He frightens you?"

"Oh, it's crazy. You wouldn't understand."

Probably not, he thought, absorbing the pain. It was nothing he hadn't heard before, but he'd wanted her to trust him, to turn to him instinctively. To see him as strong and capable and—oh, yes, as desirable, too. That most of all, perhaps.

"Probably not," he said with quiet dignity. "It's generally accepted, however, that talking a problem through helps clarify and organize the thought processes. I, um—do it myself, on occasion.''

Brilliant! Tell her how you talk to yourself. When she's done laughing at that, you can tell her about the way you sometimes watch the woman in the next apartment coming home from the supermarket, and how you pretend she's your wife, hurrying home to be with you. Oh, yes, a bit of voyeurism should instill an inordinate amount of confidence!

"That is, I sometimes try out a phrase or two aloud," he mumbled, "but only on rare occasions when I, um—have trouble consolidating my er—um . . ." He cleared his throat and tugged at his beard. If he'd been wearing a tie, he would've straightened it.

She was going to ignore him. Why shouldn't she? They were, after all, strangers. At least, *he* was a stranger. Somehow, *she* had become much more than a stranger. Electromagnetism? A biochemical reaction? Pheromones? At this point, Clement didn't really give a hang about causative factors. Whatever it was, it was happening. And it was completely outside his extremely limited experience.

He stole a look at her, noting the pure line of her profile. If there were a universal prototype for feminine beauty, he decided, it would be Martha Eberly. Withdrawing her hand from his, she lifted her head, staring over a hardwood forest that still glowed with a remnant of fall color. Watching her brought an ache to the region of his solar plexus that was oddly pleasant.

From a distance came the grinding sound of a truck straining to climb a steep grade. Clem strained along with it. *Come on. . .come on. . .this way. Look this way. Easy now, all you have to do is turn your head a bit. Just a bit more, that's it—pretend we're friends and you've something to say to me.*

Praise Paracelsus, she was going to *talk* to him!

"There's this man—Odwell..." Her voice dwindled, and Clement waited. *There was this man? Yes? And what happened?*

"He was following you," he prompted when it seemed as if she'd forgotten he was there. It occurred to him fleetingly that the more reluctant she was to talk, the more articulate he seemed to become, which in itself was a remarkable phenomenon.

"Not me—my emerald." Her gaze flew to his face, and he was struck by the sight of the slanting November sun gilding the very tips of her lashes.

"Go on," he said in what he hoped was a reassuring tone. *Her emerald?* "He was following your emerald. Uh—any particular reason?"

"Clem, do you know anything about law? I don't mean malpractice, but mining laws. Or—well, not exactly mining...*finding* laws."

"Huh?" Now which one of them was sounding incoherent? "Sorry, I'm a research chemist, not a lawyer. Naturally I've read some law, but only as a matter of interest."

"Well, maybe you can tell me— You see, I found it, but he was with me. Well, not exactly *with* me—I mean, he was a pest. He greeted every new load of diggers with this spiel about being some sort of an expert, handing out crummy business cards and offering to evaluate their finds. You know the sort of thing."

Clem didn't, but he wasn't about to say so now.

"There were plenty of samples and charts and things available—I mean, it wasn't as if any one of us expected to find anything really earthshaking. I was only along for the ride, and because it was sort of fun, and it would get me close to Hattie's, and I hadn't seen her since I moved to Louisville, but—so anyway..."

She was digressing wildly, and Clement loved every dangling, disorganized moment of it. He edged closer, close enough so that now and then he caught a drift of her fresh-bread-and-roses fragrance. She was doing remarkable things for his self-esteem, not to mention his libido. "Yes? He offered his services and then what?"

"And I said no thanks, but he turned up at the next stop, and went through the same thing. He was . . . overfriendly. You know? The sort of person you want to wash your hands after touching. A real creep."

Clement swallowed and turned to gaze over Cat Creek Valley, a shallow, laurel-filled gorge that angled diagonally down the side of the mountain. After a few moments, Martha went on speaking, and he listened, but some of the brilliance had gone out of the noonday sun. He would hear her out and advise her—help her if he could. But there was no point in pretending she could ever take someone like him seriously. And he didn't think he could survive her ridicule.

"I was on my way to the bus—you know how it gets chilly once the sun goes down—when he came up behind me and started in about showing me this place where I could find some really good stones. And when I turned around to tell him I wasn't interested—or had I already done that? I don't remember," she said distractedly. "Anyway, my shoulder bag flew off and everything got dumped, and when I was looking for my pencil—it's part of a set, and I'd just as soon lose the whole thing, but anyway, there it was. This emerald. This enormous, beautiful crystal in some sort of pinky colored rock—matrix, it's called, but I don't know if that's the name of the rock or just what they call the stuff gems come wrapped in."

Once more she fell silent. Obviously, she'd forgotten he was even there, which was just as well, because at the moment, Clem was having the devil's own time keeping his mind on her rambling tale and off her small, flawlessly constructed body.

On the other hand, he couldn't afford to jeopardize the ground he had so unexpectedly gained. It wasn't every day that a beautiful woman confided in him. Or even every decade. "This emerald. You say he's claiming it?"

"Half ownership. Because he was with me—he says—when I found it. He says there's some kind of law, which I don't for one minute believe, do you? Have you ever heard of a law like that?"

"Does this Odwell fellow have any connection, contractual or otherwise, to the property where you found the stone?"

"No way. In fact, when I complained, the proprietor of one of the mines said they all hate that sort of thing, but unless he actually breaks the law, there's not a lot they can do, since they're open to the public and he's part of it. The public, I mean."

She sighed, and Clem fought and overcame a powerful need to gather her in his arms and protect her. "He's followed you ever since?"

She nodded. "I know it's silly, but he really scares me. I can handle anything—well, almost anything—but I'm no good when it comes to dealing with . . . with crooks."

Neither was Clem. He'd never been forced to. But he was damned well going to handle this crook if it was the last thing he ever did. And if it came down to a fight, well, then . . . He would rely on his excellent reach and his knowledge of physics. Unless Odwell was taller and longer in the arms, and had a phenomenal understanding of leverage points, that should give Clem the advantage.

However, he would just as soon try logic first. "Mail it," he said decisively.

"*Mail* it! Mail what?"

"The emerald."

"Where? Back to where I found it? Thanks a lot!"

"Does it mean that much to you? Money, I mean?"

"Spoken like a rich man." Her eyes passed disparagingly over his torn shirt and stained whites. "I don't know what they pay you at that brain trust of yours, but for your information, I don't even have a job. All I've ever done is farm, keep house and take care of people, and believe me, the salary is lousy and the benefits are even worse! Don't get me wrong—I loved doing it, I really did, but now I've got to find something else. I'm twenty-nine years old and—well, anyway, that emerald just happens to be my social security, my insurance policy and my—" She shook her head. "Oh, for pity's sake, shut up, Marty," she muttered in an undertone.

"No, please. I'm interested in all you have to say."

She sent him a look of disbelief. "The point is, I need it. If I'd never laid eyes on the blessed thing, I'd have been just as happy—happier, in fact. But since I did, no crooked little weasel is going to steal it from me!"

"Then mail it. If not to your own address—"

"I don't even have an address."

"Mail it to an appraiser. I believe that would be the most logical step to take."

"Lovely. And just where do I find this person?"

He was on solid ground, at last. While he hadn't the least idea of how to go about dealing with the likes of Hubert Odwell, the wife of his secretary worked in a jewelry store in Hanes Mall. Malvern had mentioned having his mother's diamond rings appraised for insurance purposes recently by a member of the staff there.

He told her about Malvern and his wife, Virginia. "I'm sure she would be able to help."

"How do I know I can trust her?"

"Do you trust me?"

She waited so long Clem wished he could retract the question, but finally she nodded. Not effusively, but it was a definite affirmative.

Clem restrained the broad grin that threatened to break through his usual stoicism. "Well!" he said, the one word jam-packed with satisfaction.

"At least it's better than doing nothing," Martha conceded. She shook her hair, and a whiff of her fragrance reached out to him, jangling his senses until he could scarcely think coherently. Driven by the heady intoxication of success, Clem cautiously slipped an arm around her shoulders and urged her against his side.

Careful—easy does it. Scare her away now, that's the end of everything.

Her voice muffled against the clean, soapy smell of his collar, Martha said, "Look, thanks for not laughing at me. This whole crazy thing sounds like one of those wild adventure movies—women finding jewels and being chased all over two continents by wicked little men in dirty white suits who need a shave." She caught her breath. "Oops—nothing personal."

If she'd called him a registered, certified, homicidal maniac, Clem wouldn't have taken offense. He was in heaven. He was actually *holding* her! She was actually leaning her head on his shoulder, of her own free will! He felt like stepping over the mountain and handing all of Cat Creek Township to her as a gift!

"We—um—there's no reason to go to town now, I suppose," he suggested.

"No need? What do you mean, no need?"

"I mean, now that you've settled the business of what to do about Odwell and your emerald, we'll have to go back and get it, and then you can stay and wait for Hattie to come home.''

She pulled away and stared at him. "Stay? Of course I can't stay. I've still got to check on buses and find a way to get my luggage to the bus station. I appreciate your suggestion about the emerald, because frankly I didn't relish the idea of carrying it with me while I get myself settled—probably in a motel for a few days until I can get established and all. You know how flimsy those door chains are—one snip with a pair of bolt cutters and it would be hello, Hubert, goodbye, social security.''

Clem took a moment to follow her progress from Cat Creek to a motel in Winston-Salem. And while he was reasonably certain she wasn't going to find the answer to her transportation needs in a town of some thirty-seven souls, he decided to let her find it out for herself. It would allow him more time to work out a plan.

"Yes, of course," he said. Reluctantly he stood and extended a hand, which she ignored. He watched her rise as gracefully as a dryad and brush the dust from the seat of her yellow pants.

Neither of them spoke for the next two miles. The going was rough; he could hear her behind him, panting and sliding on the rocky trail. He wanted to swing her up in his arms and carry her—

Carry her somewhere where they could be alone together until he'd convinced her that they belonged together. She was the best thing that had ever happened to him in this lifetime, and she hadn't even happened. Not in any real sense.

But she was going to.

"Whew! I didn't know I was in such bad shape," she panted, pausing beside a thready little waterfall that trickled down a rocky, laurel-hung slope. Clement turned just as she scooped up a handful of water and splashed it on her face, then dipped up another palmful to drink. "This stuff's safe, isn't it? I grew up drinking from a creek that ran right through a cow pasture and lived to tell the tale."

"Unless there's a concentration of certain minerals that can be toxic when taken in excess. Or—um, extensive development higher up that isn't visible from here."

"Killjoy. It tastes great, anyway—I'll risk it. How much farther do we have to go?"

Clement didn't answer. He was too busy studying the patterns of wetness on her yellow cotton shirt—some made by perspiration, some by the recent splashing. She'd worn a sweater when they'd started out, but it had become first a cape and then an apron, worn over her hips.

Her body intrigued him. Not because it was a woman's body and most of what he knew about women's bodies had come from textbooks, but because it was hers. He found himself wanting to know everything about her—physical, mental, spiritual and emotional. And if there was something beyond those qualities, then he wanted to know about that, too. "Oh—what? Less than a mile. The other side of this ridge, then more or less directly down. First there's the creek."

"Cat Creek?"

"Yes. There's a bridge, but the creek itself is no more than a trickle. I presume the bridge was constructed for the times when the creek is in spate." Dammit, why did he always sound as if he were lecturing? "What I meant was that the creek is usually dry—"

"That's what you said."

"Not what I said—the way in which I said it. You might have noticed that I'm not an eloquent man." He held back a briar cane and waited for her to come abreast. Just as she reached him, she came to a dead stop and smiled into his eyes.

"Believe me, I'd noticed," she said gently. "You've improved enormously just since last night, though. I think you must be shy."

Terminally, he wanted to say—only somehow, not with you. And right now he seemed to be entering a new phase of his painfully slow metamorphosis. "I—uh... Catalyst," he gasped. "You, that is. I mean, people—oh, sacred Sarpedon," he muttered, and plowed ahead in silence until he was stopped by a particularly vicious cane briar that had flopped across the trail.

It caught him on the thigh and dug in. When he tried to unhook it from his pants he snagged the back of his hand and swore a little less carefully.

"Here, let me," Martha said, kneeling beside him. "Wow, you really set the hook—ah! There, that does it." She took his hand and examined it, frowning in a way that made the smiles of all other women suffer by comparison.

Clem went into cardiac arrest. By the time he'd recovered, she had cleaned his scratches with a small scrap of lace-trimmed linen and tucked it back in her pocket.

"Um... cold water. Blood stains. The creek," he stammered.

She was getting better at interpreting his non sequiturs. "It's an old hanky. It doesn't matter. Just my one-woman stand against being pushed off the planet by garbage dumps."

"Biodegradable is good," he said gravely.

"Reusable is better. Come on, let's go. If there's a bus today, I'd hate to think I missed it because I stood around arguing the merits of biodegradable over reusable." Laughing, she gave him a gentle push, and Clement had no choice but to move on.

Maybe the bridge would be out. Maybe there'd be a rock slide on the gravel road and the creek would be flooded from the rain they'd had recently and the bridge would have washed out. Then they'd be stranded together until it could be put back in order—which could take forever, as Cat Creek bridge was hardly a priority item on the agenda of the department of transportation. He doubted if the department even knew it existed.

His well of loquaciousness had dried up. When Martha's foot rolled on a stone and she recovered, laughing, Clem absorbed the heady sound of it into his bloodstream. He wondered how she'd sound played back at half speed, with all her sub- and supra-audible notes in evidence. And then, waiting for her to negotiate a particularly tricky patch of trail, he wondered how she would *look* played back at half speed.

The thought was mind-boggling.

"Clement?"

"Yes?" His voice was muffled, and she peered into his face. "Thanks for letting me talk. And for suggesting what you did. Of course, I'll probably just take it with me when I go, because nobody in his right mind would bother to follow me all the way up here. Would he?"

How would he know? He was no authority on criminal thought processes. But she needed reassurance, and he was something of an authority on that. On the need, at least. "Of course not. Logically, Odwell would be better served to stay and wait until someone else makes a find. Without appraisal, he can't know the value of your stone—it might be badly flawed. It might not even be valuable at all."

"Oh *ho*, that's all you know," she chortled. "I'll show it to you when we get back. I owe you that much."

She didn't owe him anything. What Clem wanted from her had nothing to do with her possessions. He had more

an enough to take care of them both if he never worked
nother day in his life, thanks to several rather favorable li-
ensing agreements from patents taken out before he'd gone
o work for B.F.I. Now, of course, B.F.I. had full rights to
ll his discoveries.

When he didn't respond, she swung along beside him, her
and occasionally brushing against his. Clement steeled
imself to ignore it. He was beginning to suspect he already
as in way over his head.

"You know, it's sort of funny, really," Martha mur-
ured.

"Funny?"

"Ha-ha funny, not weird funny. I mean, first I find this
abulous gemstone, and then someone tries to steal it from
e, and then I escape for help, only I end up in a place right
ff the cover of a Gothic novel, and there's this great
earded, brooding stranger who greets me with an ax, of all
hings. Dr. Barto and Mr. Hyde? I mean, it's positively
ransylvanian."

Clement didn't particularly care for the picture she'd
ainted, accurate or not. He'd thought they'd moved be-
ond the awkward beginning. "I believe Transylvania
County is southwest of here," he said with all the dignity he
ould summon.

"Oh, lighten up, Clement. Just because you're a re-
earch scientist—" And then she giggled. "A research
hemist! Oh, glory, it's perfect, don't you see? For pity's
ake, where's your sense of humor? I thought you were
Iattie's nephew. She's always saying that if you can't laugh,
ou can't love, and if you can't love, you may as well take
1 garbage."

"That makes absolutely no sense at all."

She was taking two steps to his one to keep up, and she
aught at his hand, crushing it playfully in hers. "Oh,

Clement, you know how Hattie is—she says things for effect. It's part of her style.''

He knew that. He also knew he was behaving even more like an ass than usual. From an auspicious beginning, he'd suddenly found himself back at the bottom of the heap, and he didn't even know how it had happened. Except that it was somehow connected with that infernal sensitivity of his— that horror of being laughed at that had plagued him for the past fifteen or so years.

"What's the matter," she teased gently, "don't you ever believe in laughter?"

"I'm perfectly capable of laughing when something i. genuinely amusing." God, what a stilted prig he sounded! She'd be justified in kicking his tail off the next cliff they came to.

"Well, as we've already discussed the subject of garbage, I guess it's love you don't believe in."

Suddenly he was far sweatier than the sixty-five-degree temperature and the forty-three-percent humidity could possibly account for. "There's the creek," he muttered, stepping ahead of her as if to test the narrow wooden bridge.

She caught up with him easily. Ignoring the precariousness of the ramshackle bridge, she hurried after him. "Clem, wait—darn it, I'm sorry if I touched on a tender subject, but you're not the easiest man in the world to get along with. Okay, so your love life is none of my business. Sorry I mentioned it. I was only joking, you know."

Clement wanted to shake her. He wanted to hold her in his arms and force her to stay there until he could say what was in his heart and mind. Didn't she understand, the very thought of love—the emotion she mentioned so casually— terrified him! He didn't know what it was—there was no scientific evidence it even existed. All he knew was that since yesterday—since she'd come into his life—he'd found himelf wanting something he couldn't begin to describe, and he hadn't the foggiest notion of how to go about getting it.

"You can see the roof of the post office from here," he informed her stiffly. "Watch that root up ahead—the ground drops off rather precipitously on the other side."

Martha sighed and did as she was told. She maneuvered the twisted root and the scooped out hollow just beyond it easily enough, though her mind was somewhere else. What was wrong with him? He was a strikingly attractive man—or he might be if he trimmed that beard of his. But he acted as if women were an alien species, one he might study under a microscope but would never dream of considering as equal.

Was that it? Was he another Virgil? A man who believed that a woman without a college degree and all the trappings was not to be taken seriously?

Or had a woman hurt him so badly he'd hid out here in the mountains to lick his wounds?

She could picture some women being put off by his rough exterior and his almost crippling shyness. Right at first, she'd been rather alarmed herself. But somewhere along the line the portrait of the young Clem and the tall, awkward man hiding behind a beard, an initial and a pair of thick lenses had melded into a man she'd instinctively trusted. And was fast coming to like. Like, in fact, rather a lot.

How strange. She hadn't known how she felt until she'd put it all together in her mind, but it was just as he'd said—verbalizing helped one to understand.

And then she came to an abrupt halt. "That's *it*? But where's the town?"

They had reached a badly graded road overlooking a small cluster of buildings. No more than a dozen at most. Asphalt squiggles gleamed like giant snail tracks on the surface of the narrow blacktop that ran through the middle

of Cat Creek Township. A flag hung limply outside an un
painted building that looked as if it were held together by an
assortment of faded signs.

There were three cars and four trucks in evidence. No
people. No sign of a bus or even the bread truck that had
delivered her to Hattie's house the day before.

"We can ask at the store about buses and registered
mail," Clement said. "It serves as the post office."

"It looks like one of the paintings in the dining room—all
those rooftops and the kudzu vine turning everything into
green sculpture. Are you sure this is the closest town?"

"Yes."

She gave him a suspicious look. "Have I done something
to make you angry, Clement?" For some reason, he'd
withdrawn into his shell again. Maybe she shouldn't have
teased him about his sense of humor—especially since he
didn't appear to have one.

"Angry? Of course not. If you're ready, shall we go on
down?"

Touchy. Distinctly touchy. Maybe it had something to do
with his shyness. Or his love life? Lord knows what little
time bomb she'd inadvertently tripped over. She only knew
she missed the bumbling, hesitant giant with the sweet smile
and the shy looks. She'd come to trust him. She liked him.
What's more, she'd sort of gotten the impression that he
liked her, too, but evidently she'd been wrong. It wouldn't
be the first time, nor likely the last.

"You need milk," she said. "And why not check on the
mail to see if there's any word from Hattie, as long as we're
here."

"Milk," he repeated. "Mail."

"And buses," she reminded him. Not waiting, she started
out along the steep, graveled road toward Lick Munden's
Superette.

SILHOUETTE®

 **PRESENTS**

A *Real Sweetheart of a Deal!*

**6
FREE
GIFTS**

**PEEL BACK THIS CARD AND SEE
WHAT YOU CAN GET! THEN...**

Complete the Hand Inside ➤

It's easy! To play your cards right,
just match this card
with the cards inside.

Turn over for more details ...

Incredible, isn't it? Deal yourself in right now and get 6 fabulous gifts ABSOLUTELY FREE.

1. 4 BRAND NEW SILHOUETTE DESIRE® NOVELS—FREE!

Sit back and enjoy the excitement, romance and thrills of four fantastic novels. You'll receive them as part of this winning streak!

2. A LOVELY BRACELET WATCH—FREE!

You'll love your elegant bracelet watch—this classic LCD quartz watch is a perfect expression of your style and good taste—and it's yours free as an added thanks for giving our Reader Service a try!

3. AN EXCITING MYSTERY BONUS—FREE!

And still your luck holds! You'll also receive a special mystery bonus. You'll be thrilled with this surprise gift. It will be the source of many compliments as well as a useful and attractive addition to your home.

PLUS

THERE'S MORE. THE DECK IS STACKED IN YOUR FAVOR. HERE ARE THREE MORE WINNING POINTS. YOU'LL ALSO RECEIVE:

4. FREE HOME DELIVERY

Imagine how you'll enjoy having the chance to preview the romantic adventures of our Silhouette heroines in the convenience of your own home! Here's how it works. Every month we'll deliver 6 new Silhouette Desire novels right to your door. There's no obligation to buy, and if you decide to keep them, they'll be yours for only $2.24* each—that's a savings of 26¢ per book! And there's no charge for postage and handling—there are no hidden extras!

5. A MONTHLY NEWSLETTER—FREE!

It's our special "Silhouette" Newsletter—our members' privileged look at upcoming books and profiles of our most popular authors.

6. MORE GIFTS FROM TIME TO TIME—FREE!

It's easy to see why you have the winning hand. In addition to all the other special deals available only to our home subscribers, when you join the Silhouette Reader Service, you can look forward to additional free gifts throughout the year.

SO DEAL YOURSELF IN—YOU CAN'T HELP BUT WIN!

*In the future, prices and terms may change, but you always have the opportunity to cancel your subscription. Sales taxes applicable in N.Y. and Iowa.

You'll Fall In Love With This Sweetheart Deal From Silhouette!

SILHOUETTE READER SERVICE™
FREE OFFER CARD

PLACE YOUR WINNING CARD HERE!

4 FREE BOOKS • FREE BRACELET WATCH • FREE MYSTERY BONUS • FREE HOME DELIVERY • INSIDER'S NEWSLETTER • MORE SURPRISE GIFTS

YES! Deal me in. Please send me four free Silhouette Desire novels, the bracelet watch and my free mystery bonus as explained on the opposite page. If I'm not fully satisfied I can cancel at any time, but if I choose to continue in the Reader Service I'll pay the low members-only price each month.
225 CIS JAY2
(U-S-D-09/89)

First Name		Last Name	

PLEASE PRINT

Address			Apt.

City	State	Zip Code	

Offer limited to one per household and not valid to current Silhouette Desire subscribers. All orders subject to approval.

SILHOUETTE NO RISK GUARANTEE
- There is no obligation to buy—the free books and gifts remain yours to keep.
- You'll receive books before they're available in stores.
- You may end your subscription at any time—by sending us a note or a shipping statement marked "cancel" or by returning any unopened shipment to us by parcel post at our expense.

PRINTED IN U.S.A.

Remember! To win this hand, all you have to do is place your sticker inside and DETACH AND MAIL THE CARD BELOW. You'll get four free books, a free bracelet watch and a mystery bonus.

BUT DON'T DELAY!
MAIL US YOUR LUCKY CARD TODAY!

If card is missing write to:
Silhouette Reader Service, 901 Fuhrmann Blvd., P.O. Box 1867, Buffalo, N.Y. 14269-1867

The man behind the counter stared at a spot over their heads, fly swatter in hand, and muttered an obscenity. Then he shook his head and laid down his weapon. "He'p you?" he inquired laconically.

Clement spoke up. "Mail. Milk."

"D'livery truck just left. Got in half dozen boxes o' choc'late mint ice cream. Ain't tried it, you ort to. 'S good."

"It would melt," Clement told him.

"Eat it here. I got a spoon in the back." He snatched up his swatter and went after a droning bluebottle fly, muttering threats as he rounded the scarred counter.

"No, thank you," Martha put in hurriedly. "We'd better get the mail and the milk and get on back. I—it looks like it might rain again."

The storekeeper turned to stare at her. "You with him? Up to Davenport's place? Man askin' jest yestidday who was stayin' up yonder. Told him all I knew was what I saw, and I ain't been up there since Old Man Mooney died and sold the place to a flatlander."

Martha went cold. She saw Clement's lips twitch in amusement at the order in which the events had supposedly taken place, but she was beyond appreciating the fact that he did, after all, have a sense of humor.

Odwell was still after her. Somehow, he'd managed to track her this far, and if he was nosing around Hattie's place, then he might even *be* there by now!

She pushed in front of Clement and leaned across the counter. "Do any buses come through here?"

"Nope. Nearest bus station's Asheville, I reckon."

"How far is that?" She had a sinking feeling it was *too* far.

"Straight line or road?" Lick Munden stepped over to a boxlike enclosure at one end of the cluttered counter, donned a green plastic visor and began to sort through a small bundle of mail. Martha was all but hyperventilating by the time he selected three letters, carefully putting the rest back. Then he removed the visor, hung it on a nail and came back to the center of the counter.

"Never mind about Asheville," Martha said tensely. "This man who was asking questions—was he driving a rusty blue sedan?"

"Might be. Didn't ask."

"Was he—uh—kind of short, with sandy-colored hair slicked back and a round, red face?"

The storekeeper's glance passed up the length of Clement's six-foot-four-inch frame. "Wouldn't call him perzackly tall. As to his hair, couldn't say. Wore a hat. Face 'bout as round and red as the next feller, I reckon. He weren't nobody I knowed by sight."

Clement, who had been silently observing Martha's increasing agitation, moved to stand protectively beside her. To his astonishment, he felt her small fist slip into the hollow of his palm, and he gripped it tightly. "If this man should return," he said in a tone so authoritative he barely recognized it as his own, "I would appreciate it if you wouldn't mention having seen us."

"Ain't no skin off my nose what you and your missus does. Me, I mind my own business."

Clement did his best to control the sudden rush of warmth that flooded over him at the reference to Martha as his missus. "Then you—uh—you'll respect our privacy?" he asked, forcing his features into a semblance of gravity.

"Said so, didn't I? Here's Miz Davenport's mail—milk in the cooler."

They'd barely stepped down off the stone-slab stoop when Martha said tersely, "He knows. How could he possibly know where I am? I made sure he was following the bus before I even started asking around for a ride."

"We can't be certain it's Odwell."

"No? And I suppose you're used to having people snooping around asking questions about where you are and what you're doing?"

The more upset she became, the calmer Clement grew. Who was that guy—Jack Bond? Agent double-oh something? This must be what it felt like to know one was equipped for the most hair-raising eventuality. Actually, it was quite satisfying. Downright exhilarating, in fact.

"Uh—what? Oh," he stammered, landing back on earth with a tooth-rattling thump. "No, not really, but that doesn't mean the man is Hubert Odwell."

"Of course not, it's the I.R.S. You're being audited, right?"

"Not that I know of, but I'm quite certain my accountant would—"

"Clement, get serious! You can't really be that dense, can you?"

After that jibe about his sense of humor, he couldn't resist. "My density is subject to fluctuation under conditions of stress."

She blinked, but bobbed right back. "All right, you're far from dense. Look, I'm not sure what your problem is, but whatever it is, you've got to admit that there can't be *two* strange men asking questions."

"It's conceivable."

"Which means I've got to get out of here," she said, ignoring his response.

Clem turned and clasped her shoulders, his deep-set eyes brilliant behind his rather smudged lenses. "It means nothing of the kind. No one knows where you are. Munden isn't the sort to give out free information. Besides, if you leave— if you move into a motel—who will look after you?"

Her mouth fell open as she stared up at him, and the sight momentarily robbed Clem's mind of any thoughts of emeralds and prowlers—as well as his own dismal record with women. He leaned closer. He could actually feel her breath warming his face. His mouth was dry, his hands were damp, and his heart was foundering under the strain. So close... Another few inches and his lips would touch hers.

No, dammit, another few inches and she'd be battling her way through his beard! He hadn't trimmed the thing in weeks, hadn't bothered to look in a mirror in longer than that.

"Uh—that is, yes... *well*," he said, stepping back.

"Clement, what am I going to do?" she wailed softly.

"Forget about it. For now, that is. Never worry over a problem in an untimely manner. It's exhausting and it does nothing to address the problem."

"Whew! I never know which one I'm going to be dealing with next, Barto the brilliant or Clem the closemouthed."

"Sorry—it isn't deliberate." He achieved a creditable smile, which was better than getting all stiff-necked again. He could be a real idiot when the occasion demanded—and even when it didn't. "Martha, I want you to know that you'll be quite safe with me. I've trained my body to do without sleep for thirty-six hours, and I promise you, I won't leave you unguarded for a single moment."

Martha looked at him in astonishment. "Are you serious? You *are* serious. Oh, lordy, Clement, I was only joking. It's my problem, not yours."

Struggling to determine the best way to reassure her—he could hardly tell her that he would willingly pledge the rest of his life to fulfilling her slightest whim—he said, "I make you uncomfortable. I'm aware of that, and I'm sorry, but I still intend to look after you. While you're here. Visiting with Hattie. At her house, I mean."

He gazed down at her helplessly. If she laughed—if she ridiculed his offer—he didn't know what he'd do. He was offering more than he'd ever dared offer to any woman before, more than he'd ever dreamed he could. Only how could he tell her so without frightening her even more? He'd only met her yesterday.

"Oh, Clement," Martha said softly, and she leaned her head against his chest for the briefest moment.

His heart stopped, flopped and resumed its frantic pace. Not a single one of his seven degrees could help him when it came to interpreting her smile. He only knew that no one had ever smiled at him in just that way before. Or with the same cataclysmic effect.

"You really haven't changed all that much from the boy in the portrait, have you?" she murmured, easing herself from his arms.

Six

On the way home, Clement pondered various methods of keeping Martha from finding a way to leave him. If she were determined to go, he could hardly keep her there forcibly, yet he knew he had to explore this extraordinary thing that was happening to him, and to explore it, he needed her there. Because she was at the core of it.

But how?

Threats? She could conceivably strangle while laughing at his attempts to play the tough guy. Threats were out. Bribery? What could he possibly offer that she would want, except for her freedom? Perhaps a road map and the keys to Hattie's car. Still, there had to be something he could do—some simple thing that he'd overlooked just because it *was* so simple.

Systematize, Barto. Observe, analyze, compile your data and extrapolate from there, starting with your obvious strengths and advantages.

His scowl deepened. All right then, he decided impatiently—he'd start with his *dis*advantages. That shouldn't present any problem.

One, he had problems communicating. He'd made remarkable progress since she'd come, but it still wasn't enough. He couldn't talk a fly into a sugar bowl.

Two, he had an unfortunate way of becoming aroused when he was with her, which embarrassed him and was hardly likely to instill confidence in her, should she ever become aware of it.

Numbers three through seven—he didn't have the sort of looks a woman liked in a man, his clothes were a mess, he needed a haircut and a trim and his damned glasses made him look like a myopic frog.

When he could find them, that was. He didn't even want to know what he looked like fumbling around without them.

And then it hit him. His eyes. His glasses. She'd said she hated to go off and leave him alone without them...no. That would be dishonest.

Preoccupied, he strode ahead, as if his longer legs stood a chance of catching up with the answer to all his problems.

"How about blazing a trail as you go, speedy. If I don't make it back by the end of the week, you might send out a posse—or better yet, get in touch with Hubert. We know he can always find me."

Clement waited for Martha to catch up with him. His face flaming in competition with the surrounding fall foliage, he stammered an apology. "It's the stairways. I mean, I don't care for elevators. Uh—that is—"

"If there's an elevator up this damned mountain, Clement Cornelius Barto, and you've been leading me on this chase for nothing—"

"No! That is, it's in the Grayson Building. Where I work, that is. Nine of them, and three in my apartment—floors, that is. But it's not only that—I've been doing a lot of other climbing. Mountains, I mean. Actually, not an entire one. Only portions of the same one. I think."

"Then don't let me—whew!—hold you back," Martha panted. "How about sending out a—Saint Bernard when—you get home. Or—whew! Better yet, a donkey!"

"You're exhausted."

"I'm *not* exhausted, but I've—I've got a stitch."

A stitch. "A stitch?"

"I'm tired! Winded! Pooped!" She pressed a hand against her side, and Clement closed his eyes briefly and called himself every derogatory name he could think of. "Sit on that rock." Taking her arm, he led her carefully to a worn boulder that projected above a bed of dry leaves. She sat, reminding him again of a lovely dryad, and he dropped to his knees beside her.

"Breathe naturally," he commanded, his voice rough with concern.

"That's easy for you to say!"

He gave her a few moments and then he said, "Listen."

Martha drew in several more deep breaths, wiped her brow and then looked at him expectantly, as if waiting for him to continue. "I'm listening. You're going to tell me there's a taxi stand around the corner, right?"

"Sorry. Birds."

She frowned. "Birds? Where? I don't hear any birds."

Neither did he. For once, the birds remained stubbornly silent. In all the times he'd trekked this same trail, never once had his presence stilled the cheerful cacophony that usually echoed across the ravine.

To fill the silence, he said, "I don't know their names. From their point of view, that's probably irrelevant. I've found that I like being able to hear them without having to know their names. There's a sort of..."

"There's a sort of?" she prompted when he fell silent.

"Um—well, a freedom in it. Not having to know their names, I mean. Forget it—you wouldn't understand."

"Like eating cold spaghetti for breakfast."

"Spaghetti?"

"That's freedom. When you've cooked a proper breakfast for everyone within range every single day for the past eight or ten years, and then one day you decide, what the dickens—let's all eat cold spaghetti."

His smile dawned slowly as he realized that she did indeed understand—although her metaphor was not one he would have chosen. "Right. They're spaghetti birds."

"Clement, could we open the milk? I'm parched."

He practically tripped in his haste to oblige. "I'm sorry I don't have a glass—you go first. Have all you want."

Martha laughed, and he fancied he could detect a faint echo of the sound from the dense forest surrounding them. He watched her tilt the jug, entranced with the line of her throat, the swell of her breasts and the faint shadow of her closed eyelids.

When he came to his senses again, she was holding the half-gallon jug out to him, an opalescent ring of milk showing above the bow of her upper lip. "What are you staring at?" she asked, recapping the milk and putting it down when he continued to ignore her outstretched arm.

"The turbid medium theory. Milk over pink skin. Or a red bowl. Or, um—a wood floor. Portrait painters make use of it to achieve depth in skin tones. It's what makes the sky appear to be blue when there's no blue pigment at all in the sky—only the warm light of the sun filtered through layers of atmosphere."

"What brought on all that?" Martha asked slowly.

Clem's gaze moved from her mouth to her eyes and back again. "The milk. Around your mouth."

The tip of her tongue darted out to circle her lips, leaving behind a sheen of moisture, and suddenly, his breathing grew labored. He shifted his position.

"Stop staring at me that way! Am I breaking out or something?"

"Martha, um . . . do you like kissing?"

She almost fell off her perch. "Do I like *what*?"

"I'm sorry, I shouldn't have asked that."

"Probably not, but you did. What I want to know is . . . why?"

"Why what?"

She stood abruptly, and her foot struck the milk jug, toppling it several feet down the trail. "Clement, what is it with you? First you can't talk at all, and then you spout off like a textbook on the wildest assortment of topics, and then you—you sound like a—an I don't know what! How old are you, anyway?"

"Thirty-two and a quarter." He was standing, too, his face a study in consternation. "I shouldn't have asked you that."

"You're certainly old enough to know better. A man doesn't go around asking strange women if they—well, you know. Or maybe you were joking?"

"No. Well, do you?" he persisted doggedly.

"Of course I do! That is, sometimes I do. Oh, for goodness sake, it all depends."

"On what?"

The sun slanted through a break in the trees, highlighting a patch of wildflowers, an eroded granite outcropping and one extremely dusty plastic jug of milk. Clement stared at them unseeingly. One foot dug a shallow furrow in the path. She was right. It was a stupid question, and he was old enough to know better. Thank God he hadn't come right out and asked her if she enjoyed the physical act of love. Because he really wanted to know. What he wanted to know even more was if she enjoyed it enough to risk doing it with him.

Oh, lord, this was getting out of hand! He couldn't even talk to the woman without making a fool of himself, and already he was worrying about how he was going to go about making love to her!

In fact, he was worrying so much he was becoming acutely uncomfortable. Physically. This was embarrassing! The last time he'd suffered such pronounced symptoms had been when Danforth's secretary had come by to pick up his requisitions and noticed a run in her panty hose. She'd proceeded to investigate the source right there in his laboratory. She'd kept sending him funny looks, as if daring him to do something. What had she thought he could do about it, produce a fresh pair out of a test tube?

This time he couldn't very well relieve the immediate physical manifestations by running down nine flights of stairs to the coffee machine in the basement and back up again.

"On how I feel about someone, of course."

The words startled Clem from his mental miasma. She was obviously responding to something he'd said, but what? He did some quick backtracking, matching question to answer, and ended up feeling more discouraged than ever. Her feelings toward him were clear enough. The kindest thing would be to let her go, although he wasn't quite sure how to go about it short of calling a cab from town to drive her to the airport as Hattie had done.

"I'm sorry," he mumbled.

"Sorry for what?"

Forcing a smile he didn't feel, he explained. "Logjams. Sometimes big chunks break through, sometimes small trickles. Actually, my thought processes are remarkably clear. They just get muddied up somehow in translation."

He waited for her to laugh. Or to call him a nerd, a nut case or any of the usual terms he was accustomed to hearing. Usually, but not always, spoken in an undertone. He'd actually thought he was improving, but it wasn't going to work.

"You're talking about your shyness—the way you sometimes seem to have trouble making yourself understood."

"Sometimes? That's like saying it sometimes snows in Siberia."

But Martha was beginning to understand this great, woolly teddy bear. Right now he was all bent out of shape because he'd blurted out a sophomoric question about kissing. And because he was aroused. If he even suspected she'd noticed that, he'd have turned every color of the rainbow instead of merely red.

Lord knows, if it had happened when he'd first confronted her with that ax in his hands, she'd probably have sailed right off that cliff at the edge of the road. She wasn't cut out to be a sacrificial maiden. But since then, she'd come to know him better. And the really shocking thing was that his physical reaction didn't shock her at all. Just the opposite, in fact. She found it almost stimulating. All right—she'd found it *extremely* stimulating.

Martha had entertained a few sexual fantasies of her own when she hadn't been too exhausted with having to work on the farm, look after Papa, go to school and study art in her spare time. A good many of them had even been about this very man. Or rather, about a brooding young man in an unforgettable portrait.

But she was an adult now, and she'd learned the hard way that fantasies were strictly a hothouse product. They withered fast in the cold air of reality.

As Clem and Martha sat on the rock together, steeped in the fragrance of resinous forest and sun-dried grasses and wildflowers, Martha's sexual awareness gradually began to fade, to be replaced by something more easily acceptable. Certainly a lot more comfortable.

The old tenderness she'd felt for Hattie's portrait had returned full force, with overtones of something deeper, richer, warmer. A moment's nostalgia, brought on by all the rush and confusion of the past few weeks, she told herself. Hardly surprising after all she'd been through. It was quiet and peaceful here, and Clem was a comforting, undemanding presence beside her. Almost too undemanding.

Suddenly Martha, who had never in her life asked a man out, never called first or kissed on a first date—or even *had* that many dates, at least as far as variety was concerned—felt a sudden, startling urge to turn and take C. Cornelius Barto in her arms, to succor him, to smooth that unruly forelock from his face and—if she could find a mouth under all that beard—to kiss it!

Whoa, lady! Both feet on the ground! She could hear her father's voice as if he were right there beside her, and she heeded the voice of caution by force of habit.

Coercing her protesting muscles into action, she said, "I reckon we'd better get moving. I'm not even sure I can get up."

While she was trying to convince her leg muscles that it was their duty to lever her butt off the rock, Clement arose with a lithe movement that could have made her hate him. Was it her fault that housework and keeping up with two small dynamos didn't exactly put her into Jane Fonda condition? Just because *he* could leap tall buildings in a single bound...

Except for a few groans, a grunt or two and a lot of huffing and puffing, the journey continued in silence. Martha allowed her mind to drift, too tired to call it to heel. It drifted frequently to Clement Barto. Slightly less frequently to Hubert Odwell—she was really going to have to settle matters with him, and she wasn't quite convinced that getting the emerald out of her possession would do it. What if he didn't believe her? They never did in the movies.

The sun was grazing the tops of the trees on the western side of the ridge by the time they sighted the house. Martha, doing her best to ignore screaming muscles and swollen feet, muttered, "If by some miracle...I make it as far as the bathtub, I'm going to...take up residence there for the next two weeks. Whew! I warn you, Clement...don't even try to evict me for anything short of a...four-course dinner!"

Clement grinned at the slight figure plodding up the last stretch. "Eggs or cans?"

A scathing look told him what she thought of her choices. "Just keep an eye out...for buzzards circling overhead, will you? And next time you need milk..."

He could hear her labored breathing, see the look of exhaustion on her face, and even sweaty, dusty and flushed with exertion, she was the most beautiful creature he had ever beheld, real or imaginary. Suddenly infused with fresh energy, he said, "Your emerald. We'll have to go back to mail it."

"Don't even think about it." Martha groaned, pausing to eye the last uphill stretch. "Clem, I've been doing some thinking..." Leaning against a locust tree, she waited for him to join her. "Slow up, darn it! You've walked circles around me and—" Pant, gasp. "You're not even breathing hard! What are you grinning about, you hairy hyena? If you're waiting for me to fall at your feet, forget it. I might be a weakling, but I'm a proud weakling."

Clem's laughter echoed off the surrounding slopes. When he could speak again, he did his best to salve her ego. "You're just not used to the altitude."

"This isn't exactly...Mount Mitchell. A few years ago...I could have kept up with you...but I...must have gotten soft."

"Soft," he repeated, and the thought of her softness had an immediate and not unexpected effect on him.

"In the body, not the head," she retorted. "Soft meaning weak—not soft as opposed to hard. Although I guess— oh, forget it!"

He only wished he could! Hunching his shoulders protectively, Clem drew one knee up, bracing his foot on the rough bark. He forced himself to think of cold showers, icy mountain streams. When that didn't work, he turned his mind to one of the more fascinating projects he'd had to sideline when he had taken over Danforth's administrative duties.

Unfortunately, his senses had a mind of their own, and they were reveling in the sweet-spicy fragrance of her heated body, the zephyr sound of her breathing. He thought of the milk that had rimmed her lips and licked his.

Soft as opposed to hard. God! The very concept sent him reeling!

She broke through his feverish daydream, scattering the pieces before he could snatch them back. "If you're still waiting for me to keel over, forget it," she said dryly. "Just give me another minute...to catch my breath...and I'll race you to the front door."

Clem prided himself on his fast recovery. "I'll even give you a head start, since you're handicapped."

"Oh, for pity's sake, I am not! My feet hurt, that's all."

"No, I meant your legs."

Bottom against the tree, Martha leaned out, twisting around so that she could glare at him. "What's wrong with my legs?"

"They're too short. I mean, they're quite sufficient—that is, they're certainly in proportion—" With a short oath, he turned and swept her off the ground mail, milk and all. "I haven't even seen your legs—" Yet, he qualified silently. "But I'm sure mine are longer."

Martha registered a single squawk of protest then sagged in his arms, and Clem savored the moment. He almost hated to begin the journey. Once begun, it would quickly end. On the other hand, holding her this way was having a rather predictable physiological effect. Cold sweat. Palpitations. Dry mouth. Etcetera.

He started walking. And then he started worrying. What if he tripped? What if he gave in to the overpowering need to lower her to the ground and kiss every square—and rounded—inch of her marvelous body, short legs included?

He felt an arm slide around his neck and he trembled. Common sense told him that she was merely anchoring herself in case he dropped her, but then, common sense was one area in which he'd always been lamentably weak. If it couldn't be taught in a classroom or a laboratory—and that particular commodity couldn't—then he hadn't learned it, because he'd wasted ninety percent of his life in one or the other.

At first she was stiff. Laughing, she demanded to be set down, but bit by bit she ceased protesting and began to relax. Before Clem had gone a third of the way, her cheek was resting in the curve of his shoulder, making him feel handsome, charming and every bit as masterful as Petruchio at his best.

"Watch that root. If you fall, I fall," Martha said a little breathlessly, and his arms tightened imperceptibly. Ease up, you fool, he cautioned himself silently. Don't scare her now—not when things are just beginning to look promising.

Not until they were at the front door did Clement reluctantly set her down. She sighed and promptly kicked off both her shoes. He was tired, too, but he would have held her willingly for the next fifty years if he could have thought of an excuse that sounded even faintly reasonable.

He seriously doubted that she would care for the real one—that he could never remember anything having felt so wonderful, so right, in his entire life as she did. In his arms. Pressed tightly against his body, her sweet scent warming his nostrils, her lips so close he could have touched them with his if he'd dared.

One day soon he would dare, he promised himself. Somehow, he would learn whatever had to be learned— there were books, weren't there? There were how-to books on everything these days. And once he felt sufficiently knowledgeable, he would ask her—

Ask her what? Hell, he didn't even know the questions, much less the answers!

But he could learn. He had a brain. What was the use of having spent his entire life in pursuit of knowledge if he hadn't learned how to achieve the one thing he wanted more than anything else in the world?

Shouldering open the screen door, Clem busied himself with the massive pewter latch. Dream on, you great blundering ox. And what's she going to be doing while you bone up on the gentle art of wooing a woman?

"Need some help? What's the matter, can't you find the right key?"

"No. Yes."

"Oh, for pity's sake," she muttered tiredly, leaning against the wall, the jug of milk dangling from her fingertips.

Clement was actually trembling by the time he felt the latch give way. He reached out to relieve her of the milk and accidentally knocked it from her grasp. And then he swore softly.

It was Martha who retrieved the milk. Taking his hand in her other one, she led him inside and shut the door. "Men! You're as bushed as I am, only you're too proud to let on. Well, don't be embarrassed—you don't have to prove anything to me. I'm ready for a long hot soak, and then I'm going to dig out my slippers, because I don't think I'll be able to cram my feet into real shoes for a week at least. Next time I start out on an eight-mile hike, I hope someone ties me to a tree."

Taking the guilt for her suffering upon his own shoulders, Clem searched the cluttered files of his mind for something to offer in assuagement. "Soak. Maybe powder—salts? I'm not sure of the proper treatment—"

"Don't worry, I'm going to soak. If I'm not out by Thanksgiving, save me some turkey."

"I promise, I won't even open the can until you're out of the bathroom." His smile was tentative, and his heart soared when she chuckled in response to his feeble joke.

Actually, Clement could have done with a bath himself, but he would have to wait, thanks to the peculiarities of the antiquated hot-water system. Waiting for Martha was a privilege. He would willingly commit to a lifetime of cold showers if he thought it would add to her comfort.

In fact, for his own comfort, he would probably have to. "You go ahead," he said. "I have a something that needs attending to first."

It had been a mistake, Clem admitted to himself some half hour later when he tried to get up from the floor. The minute she'd gone upstairs, he'd stretched out on the rug on his stomach, knowing full well what would happen if he fell asleep in that position. And then he'd fallen asleep.

It had happened. He could barely turn his head.

Levering himself up by degrees, he winced at the assortment of twinges and kinks in his cervical region. That was the part of his spine that caught hell. Too many years spent poring over books and microscopes. Plus the tension. That always got him in the neck.

Using a crawling, sliding technique, he made it as far as the ottoman and then he braced himself to do what had to be done. Head hanging, he laced his fingers together at the back of his neck and began manipulating.

"Another headache?" Martha said from the doorway.

Ducking around, he squinted in the direction of her voice, having removed his glasses for safekeeping. The movement was too much for his spasming muscles, and he groaned. "Stiff neck."

"Need some help? Jack used to collect tension back there from hanging over his books too long. He has rotten posture." She was beside him before he realized it, her hands sliding underneath his. Clem reached for his glasses just as she dug in her thumbs, and she said, "Uh-uh. Leave them off. Hang your head forward and relax, I won't hurt you."

Jack? Who was Jack? Why had she been in a position to offer this sort of service to him? "Ouch!" He yelped when she hit a tender spot.

"Hurt? Good. It means I'm in the right area. I'll loosen you up back here and get the blood flowing again."

"Your hands are stronger than they look."

"I grew up on a farm. I was priming tobacco and milking before I was old enough to read."

"Who's Jack?" Clem's voice was muffled, his head hanging practically onto his chest, but it was working. He could feel the spasms beginning to ease. Her hands were remarkably effective.

"My brother. I've been living with him for the past few years, taking care of my niece and nephew. Jack's a widower." Her thumbs lifted and soothed, lifted and soothed, firmly, but without bruising force. "Trina died when Jenny was born, and I went out to Louisville and—that still hurt? No? Good. Anyway, three weeks ago Jack remarried. I stayed while they went on their honeymoon, and now I'm on my way home. I was going to have a little vacation and visit Hattie on the way, but you know what happened then."

He knew. Yet he didn't know anything at all. He wanted to know everything about her. What she read, what music she listened to—if she liked rainy days and cold winter mornings, or blue skies and burnished summer sunrises.

"Ah," Clement groaned. She was working down his spine, the heel of her hands pressing hard and twisting. He could feel a rush of heat mounting in his body that had nothing at all to do with her hands on his back—nothing and everything, he amended. She had the same effect on him simply by being in the same room.

Relaxed after her bath, Martha seemed inclined to talk. "I'll miss the children. I've tried not to think about it because I know it's best for Jack and the kids this way—a regular family, with both parents. But I've had Jenny since birth. She's like my own child. Poor Jack—he and Trina married right out of high school—probably too young, but you know how it is."

That was just the trouble. He didn't know how it was. Hadn't an inkling. He did know, however, that the thought of being married to a woman—to *this* woman—of giving her children . . .

Well, it was quite simply the most wonderful thing imaginable in a large and wondrous universe. He would have traded any number of Nobel prizes for a woman of his own. Not just any woman, but *this* woman.

"So this is the way it comes about," he mused aloud.

"The way what comes about? Am I being too rough on you? Sorry. You're so big. I mean your muscles—your shoulders, that is." She stammered to a halt and went on kneading.

How love comes about. How it manifests itself, Clem thought. He almost spoke the words aloud, but caught himself in time. He hadn't believed in love since he'd been fifteen, in spite of the fact that a large portion of the world's literature was based on just such a hypothesis.

Love. He'd considered it a myth, at best—rationalization for the procreative urge, at worst. Other children had believed in the tooth fairy—in Santa Claus. Clem never had. He'd been inclined to suspect a mutant virus whenever he'd seen otherwise sane men and women suddenly lose all semblance of reason over a member of the opposite sex.

"'Love, like a mountain wind upon an oak, Falling upon me, shakes me leaf and bough,'" he murmured wonderingly.

"What?"

Face flushed, he fumbled for his glasses and jammed them on his face. "Um—it's—uh . . . Sappho. Uh, something she said. Wrote, that is. I—um—don't know why it popped into my head. Mountain wind. I expect the wind blowing reminded me of it."

"There's not a whiff of wind," Martha retorted, but her voice was not quite as sharp as it might have been. In fact, it sounded almost gentle when she said, "Clement, do you realize we didn't have any lunch today, and now it's almost eight o'clock? I don't know about you, but I've already worked off a week's worth of calories.''

He pounced on the excuse. ''Hunger. That's it!''

''Why don't you go get a nice, warm soak to finish what I started here while I fix us some supper? Say, forty-five minutes? Will that be enough time for you to get the rest of the kinks out?''

He was not a tub man, he realized some fifteen minutes later, immersed in hot water up to just below his sternum. Why hadn't he settled for a quick shower? A cold one, at that?

Because she'd told him to get in the tub. If she'd told him to climb into an autoclave and switch it on, he would have cheerfully steamed himself purple. This business of being in love was going to be tricky! It might even be fatal if he didn't learn how to handle it.

Thoughtfully, Clem scrunched down deeper, resting his heels on the brass and porcelain sprockets of the faucets. By George, he had to admit, it did feel pretty good. There was something downright intimate about sharing a bathtub, even if they shared it at different times. He could still smell the spicy, flowery scent of whatever it was she used—soap or shampoo or whatever. Her toiletries were arranged neatly on the marble basin—a bottle with yellow roses on it. A jar with a yellow lid. A lavender razor and a pink toothbrush. Intimate things. Who else knew the color of her toothbrush and razor?

Suddenly, Clem's mind took off on a tangent that sent the blood coursing through his body. His pulses hammered at the mental images that were forming faster than he could deal with them in the steamy atmosphere.

There's no reason two people can't share a bathtub at the same time, if one of them sits . . .

He shook his head. No, not that way. He'd want to see her face and her breasts, not the back of her head and her scapulae. But if she turned around to face him, then where would her legs go? Crossed over his thighs? Along his flanks? In the short, old-fashioned tub, there wasn't room to lie down, even for one. With two people involved, one of them was either going to drown or break a few bones.

To hell with hot soaks! He was going to be in worse shape than ever if he didn't get his mind on something a little less stimulating. A few fractures were beginning to sound like a reasonable price to pay for holding Martha's wet and warm body against his and allowing nature to take its course.

Hastily, Clem pulled the plug, drained half the water out and turned on the cold water full force. Five minutes later, he rubbed himself ruthlessly with a coarse towel and then dressed, popping another button and momentarily jamming his zipper in his haste.

The prosaic smell of coffee greeted him as soon as he opened the door, and he began to breathe easier. Was that ham he smelled cooking? It occurred to him that part of his hallucinations might be due to the fact that his body had not been refueled in some time.

But the scientist in him refused to allow him to get away with such faulty reasoning. His brain might have wandered off the track, but his body knew very well what it wanted. And it wasn't food.

"It's ham and cheese omelets, and they're done. There's cheese toast, too. Sorry if that doesn't suit, but I didn't have a whole lot to pick from. You don't have any butter."

She was still wearing her robe. It was yellow, belted at the waist, made of some soft, corded fabric—chenille, he thought, and he wondered what she was wearing underneath. Hoping the flush he could feel rising up from his collar would stop at his beard line, Clem took his seat at the

head of the table with as much aplomb as he could muster.
Unfortunately, his newly discovered talent for creating erotic
fantasies was making it rather difficult. Damn those books
of Hattie's!

Clearing his throat, he said, "The word comes from the
French word for caterpillar, you know."

Martha looked startled. "Omelet? I thought it had
something to do with eggs."

There went his foot again. "Um—chenille. Your, uh—
whatchamacallit. Robe. The word omelet comes from the
Latin word for small plate."

"How . . . interesting," she said faintly, picking up her
fork.

"No, it's not." Clement took up his utensils, holding the
knife in one hand and the fork in the other, as though they
were weapons. "I don't know anything interesting. That
is—everything I say comes out sounding like recycled textbooks. Or worse."

"That's not true, Clem. And anyway, it's no great crime.
Besides, you're getting better all the time, honestly. Now eat
your toast while it's hot. Cold cheese toast is stringy and
tasteless."

Obediently, he picked up his cheese toast and took a large
bite, feeling as if he were back in the nursery.

"I added a pinch of cocoa to the coffee." Martha cupped
her mug in her hands, inhaled and sipped. "I wanted something rich-tasting tonight. We've earned it, don't you think
so?"

"That was kind of you."

"It wasn't kind at all," she said impatiently. "I did it because I like it! For all I know, you could be allergic to cocoa." She attacked her omelet, releasing even more of its
rich, enticing aroma.

Gradually the stiffness left him. So he'd done it again. Overreacted. It wasn't the first time, and it would hardly be the last. He simply wasn't a social creature, and the sooner he stopped trying to be something he wasn't, the better for all concerned.

Clem felt considerably more comfortable. His stomach, at least, was satisfied. Martha was a relaxing companion. She didn't chatter, nor did she demand of him things that were beyond his capability.

In a way, he almost wished she would.

Blotting his shaggy mustache with a napkin, he managed an apologetic smile. "I'm afraid I need a trim rather badly. Packing—I don't travel much. I forgot some things . . ."

"I noticed. You're welcome to one of my razors. I have a bag of disposable ones in my toilet case. So much for my stand on ecology," she said with a rueful smile, which he found totally endearing. "Frankly, I was hoping you'd shave while I was here, now that I know who you are. I'm curious to see how much you've changed since Hattie painted that portrait."

Clement's coffee spoon clattered against his saucer. "You know about the portrait?"

She nodded. "For at least the past ten or twelve years. I used to go home with Hattie for lunch sometimes on Saturdays, since I lived out in the country and came in for morning and afternoon classes."

"I'm surprised you recognized me under all this." Clem tugged at a length of curly, reddish-brown beard.

"I didn't at first, but things began to add up. Your name. Your eyes. Something about the way you hold your head—sort of watchful. Like you don't quite trust people."

"I was only sixteen or so," he muttered, embarrassed at her analysis.

"It's a beautiful portrait, Clem. You must be awfully proud of Hattie."

When he didn't reply, she smiled down at her plate and said, "I know she was awfully proud of you. You were the only one of her family she ever talked about. She said you were a genius, but even so, there was an outside chance for you. I never did know what she meant. I'm afraid at that age, I did more looking than listening."

Clement fiddled with a crust of cheese toast, strewing crumbs on the table and knocking his fork to the floor. He mumbled something about the weather.

"What?"

"Nothing!" he practically yelled, and then wished he could evaporate without a trace. "Sorry. I didn't mean to shout."

They sipped coffee silently for a few moments, and Clem searched for a tactful way to ask something that had occurred to him while he was hunting down a pair of hole-free socks.

Was she free? Had she already formed an attachment to any particular man? Did she believe that two discerning adults could meet and instantly recognize qualities in the other that would be a sound basis for a lasting relationship?

Would she lie down with him and let him hold her in his arms, and allow him to make love to her again and again until he finally learned how to please her?

Suddenly he leaped to his feet, tipping his chair and catching it just before it toppled over. "Wait here! I mean, excuse me, please."

Her look of concern would have thrilled him if he hadn't already turned away. "Clement, what's wrong? Are you ill?"

"Wait right there. Don't move! I'll be back in five minutes."

Martha stared at his half-eaten omelet. She wasn't exactly a gourmet chef. Still, no one had ever reacted quite this violently to her cooking before.

Maybe he was allergic. Not to eggs, because they'd had those before. To cocoa? Possibly.

Or to her.

Seven

The scissors were right where he remembered having seen them—in Hattie's sewing basket. And while they weren't exactly regulation shears, they would do well enough in an emergency. This was an emergency. He walked into the bathroom and closed the door behind him. Clement frowned at his image in the mirror. He angled his head this way and that, and then grabbed a handful of beard. No wonder she'd been staring at him earlier. His face looked like the backside of a hedgehog.

And these clothes! Everything he owned had shrunk since he'd been in Cat Creek. Something to do with the water, no doubt. The seams of all his shirts were giving way.

Clement had never given much thought to clothes, other than to wish the laundry wouldn't use so much starch. He limited himself to safe combinations of black, gray, tan and white, according to the season. On the rare occasions when Hattie barged into his life and commandeered him for dinner or an opening, he wore one of the suits she'd picked out for him. His shirts were all of the finest quality. And they all were white. His ties were a blend of silk and wool, and like his socks, they were all black. It was a safe system.

Denim. That was what he needed, he told himself for the second time in as many days. Even old Heinrich, a legend in bioastronautics in his day, lived in denim pants and something that looked like a pair of red pajamas. A running suit, he called it. On Heinrich it looked more like an empty Christmas stocking hanging from a doorknob.

It also looked a hell of a lot more comfortable than over-starched whites or khakis, Clement conceded, making up his mind to augment his limited wardrobe the very first chance he got.

Ten minutes later, he stood frowning at the reflection of his unfamiliar face, parts of which had not seen the light of day in several years. As barbering tools, a disposable razor and a pair of pinking shears left something to be desired, but they'd done the job. He now sported half a dozen nicks, a ragged but manageable mustache and a clean-shaven, if somewhat pale, jaw. Should he have rid himself of the mustache, too? Without the beard, it was too obvious. It seemed to have no purpose other than adornment, and Clem was acutely uncomfortable with the idea of adorning himself.

However, he couldn't quite bring himself to bare his entire face. Besides, the real test was not what he thought of it, but what Martha would think. Would she consider it an improvement? Or would she take one look at his bare face and start laughing?

Oh, hell, it had been a lousy idea! He should have known better. A clean-shaven jaw wasn't going to improve his ability to converse in a suave and debonair manner. That took years of practice, starting, no doubt, in kindergarten.

At five years old, he'd been exploring the fascinating worlds of algebra, astronomy and chemistry, not dancing around the maypole with some pigtailed tadpole in pink ruffles. Nor had he managed to catch up since.

How was he supposed to know what women liked to talk about? Women who weren't involved in his own area of interest, that was. Music? The mathematics upon which some of the major compositions were based was a remarkably fascinating topic—but what if she didn't care for music?

There was always poetry. No! Scratch poetry. Those lines of Sappho's he'd blurted out earlier had embarrassed him and done nothing at all for her. Maybe she preferred the French poets.

Flowers! All women liked flowers, didn't they? He knew a lot about flowers—botanical names, chemical properties... If they got stuck for a topic, he could always bring in botany. Maybe he'd ask her why she smelled like roses and fresh-baked bread instead of chemicals, musk and dry-cleaning fluid, like most other women.

Hearing a sound outside the door, Clement swallowed hard and gripped the edge of the sink. When it came to conversation, he'd just have to allow her to take the lead. Surely it couldn't be that difficult to carry on a casual conversation. They'd been doing great for a while today.

"Go get 'em, tiger!" he growled at the stranger in the mirror. "Concentrate hard on being casual and spontaneous. Nothing to it!" He raised a fist in a mock salute.

"Clement, are you all right?"

The fist fell and sweat suddenly beaded his forehead. Hell, no, he wasn't all right! He was coming apart at the seams, both figuratively and literally. What's more, he hadn't the foggiest notion of what to do about it. "Right. Uh—I mean, I am. Yes!" *Smooth, Barto—real smooth!*

He flung open the door before he could lose his nerve and then winced at her startled gasp. She didn't like his face. His damned nose was too long, and his jaw was too—too something. "I'm sorry. I thought it would be an improvement," he mumbled. Stepping back, he tried to close the door again.

"C.C. Barto, don't you dare shut that door in my face!" She had her foot in it. Short of sacrificing a few of her slipper-clad metatarsi, there was nothing he could do.

Reluctantly, Clem allowed her to look her fill. Nothing—not even the tandem bout of walking pneumonia that had landed him up here in Buncombe County in the first place—had ever made him feel quite so vulnerable. "I'm sorry. I've startled you."

"No, you— That's not it."

"I shouldn't have. It was a bad idea." He covered his chin with his hand. "Er, um—it was bothering me. With summer coming on and all..." *It's November, cretin!*

Before he could duck inside the bathroom, Martha reached up and brushed her hand down the side of his nude face. Adrenaline pumped through his system. "I wondered if you'd changed," she murmured.

"Changed?" He sounded as if he were strangling. He *felt* as if he were strangling. Her hands were so soft, so...

"From the portrait."

They were standing in the doorway. Behind them was the bathtub where he'd lain fantasizing about her. This was no place to hold a discussion—even Clement was smart enough to know that much. Edging her out into the hall, he leaped on the opening she'd offered. "The portrait! I mean, art. In general, that is. Do you like it? Or would you rather have a cup of coffee?"

Martha's smile trembled on the verge of laughter. The good kind of laughter, filled with tenderness, caring and empathy. All those things she had no business feeling at this stage. It was too soon. Clement was too... different.

Besides, her plans were all made, and they definitely didn't include an involvement with a sweet, slightly dippy hermit, no matter how appealing he was. "Coffee would be nice," she said huskily, "and yes, I've always been interested in art, but..."

It was only a matter of inches. Later, Martha was never certain which one of them had closed the distance. It was as if they were being drawn together by a giant magnet, each one too mystified by the process to do anything about it.

Clement stopped breathing. He wasn't sure, but he thought perhaps his heart might have ceased beating for several moments. He lowered his head, and Martha lifted hers, and he felt her breath touch his lips like a phantom kiss... like a dream.

Only dreams didn't wind their arms around him and stroke his back. Dreams didn't feel cool for one split instant and then melt in his arms, turning him incandescent... and decidedly tumescent.

Their lips met—slid, met again. Clem pressed hard and then drew back, afraid of hurting her. His teeth—her teeth—lips were incredibly sensitive. He broke away, gasping for breath, but he couldn't stay away, and this time he had to know—would it shock her? Would she be repelled?

He had to know how she tasted. He was starving for her.

Instinct carried him tentatively into the kiss—a gentle parting of the lips, a hesitant touch of the tongue, and then the kiss gathered its own momentum, carrying him to a depth that was way over his head. He couldn't get enough of her—the taste, the feel—the very essence of her. His chest was bursting, he was trembling all over, beset by the fierce demands of a body that knew what it wanted and would not be thwarted by mere reason.

The soft chenille cocoon fell away unnoticed. Two of the remaining four buttons on Clem's shirt landed on the carpet. His bare chest strained against the rumpled yellow batiste of her gown, his hands searching out treasure after treasure, marveling over the incredible phenomenon that was Martha Eberly.

His glasses were worse than useless, and he flung them away. Driven wild by the exquisite agony of desire, he came to his senses only enough to realize that he'd been moving his pelvis in such a way, pressing himself against her so that she couldn't mistake what was happening to him.

He was horrified. She must despise him! Making a heroic effort to control his need, he tried to explain, to apologize. "Martha, I—"

"No, don't."

With rough, unsteady hands, he held her away. And then brought her back to him, crushing her fragile femininity against his crude masculinity one last time before he put her away from him. "So sorry, my dearest one," he muttered. "I can't tell you how sorry I am."

She fumbled at the neck of her gown. "Oh, no, it was—I shouldn't have—" Groping frantically for her robe, she tried to think of something that would explain her inexplicable lapse of judgment with a man she'd met only the day before. She knew better, she honestly did. In this day and age—and she was no kid! The trouble was, he was so entirely outside her realm of experience that she didn't know how to deal with him. She'd dropped her guard, and it—whatever *it* was—had hit her before she could duck!

Spotting a glow of pale yellow against the faded pattern of the hall runner, she dived for it at the same moment Clement did. They collided, he steadied her then backed away as if he'd burned his hands.

He looked so full of self-reproach, and Martha, her heart constricting painfully, knew it was going to be up to her to navigate them safely through the next few moments. She tied on her robe, then, spotting his glasses against the baseboard, retrieved them and placed them in his hand. "Clement, have you ever considered getting contacts?"

"Hm—the thing is . . . Contacts? Oh, I—ah . . ."

"Don't tell me, I already know. You can't hide behind contacts, right?" With a sigh she watched as he hurriedly rammed the patched and fingerprinted glasses into place.

Both feet on the ground, Marty. She simply couldn't allow herself to be sidetracked just because she'd run headlong into an old fantasy figure and found him more fascinating than ever. That was all it was, really. It couldn't be anything more, because they didn't know each other, and if you didn't know someone, you couldn't possibly fall in love with them. Infatuation, maybe, but not love.

"Coffee would be nice," she said, forcing herself to a calmness she was far from feeling. In unspoken agreement, they headed for the kitchen. "And yes, now that you mention it, I've always been interested in art. I was never all that good at it, but one of these days, when I have time for a hobby, I plan to take it up again. It's the least I can do, after Hattie invested all that time and effort on me."

Clement was grateful that one of them, at least, had found the way back down to earth. He still had a ways to go yet, but he would follow her lead. She hadn't slugged him. She hadn't laughed in his face. That was a good sign, wasn't it?

"The—uh—relationship between the mathematical basis for certain paintings and some of the major musical compositions is—um, interesting, don't you think so?" He made a pass at his untidy hair and then tried surreptitiously to tuck in his shirttail.

"I'll take your word for it." She rinsed out the coffeepot and filled it with water while Clem took down two cups and two saucers, none of which matched.

His head was still spinning. Had he really kissed her the way he thought he had? Long, hungry kisses? Tongue-searching, teeth-touching kisses? The sort he'd read about in novels? He'd always discounted nine-tenths of the male-female thing as sheer imagination, but it seemed he'd been wrong. If anything, the authors hadn't done their subject justice.

"—because math was never one of my favorite subjects," Martha was saying. "My best classes were art and literature—the inexact sciences, you might say. Although I was good at spelling, too, and that's sort of an exact science."

"It's illogical."

"I know—it's fluky, but I won all the spelling bees, anyway. Well, not all, but most of them. So I thought I'd try nurse's training and maybe later on take up art as a hobby." She spoke rapidly, as if she were trying to fill up the silence. "I never really had enough talent as an artist to make a living at it, and I think it's much better to be a first-rate something practical than a fourth-rate something *im*practical, don't you?"

Her smile was too brilliant to be entirely true. Even in his dazed state, Clem recognized that much. She was nervous, and it was all his fault, and he was sorry, but he didn't think it would help matters much if he told her that she could never be a fourth-rate anything because she was unique. Superb. All the superlatives in the five languages in which he was fluent fell short of describing the wonder and beauty of Martha Eberly.

However, she was obviously waiting for a response of some kind. Clem reached back through the fog and grasped at a straw. "Spelling. I didn't mean you were illogical, I meant that spelling was."

"Oh."

The silence was broken by a rumble of thunder, and a new tension seemed to fill the air. Clem hunched his shoulders, shifted from one foot to the other and in desperation blurted out the first thing that entered his mind. "Are you—um, attached or anything? To a man, I mean?"

She dropped the measuring spoon, scattering coffee over the counter. "Now look what you made me do!" Sweeping the mess into her palm, she dumped it in the trash, still grumbling. "Now I've lost count."

Doggedly, Clement persisted. He had to know. "Are you?"

"No, I am definitely not attached. To a man or anything else!"

"Good." Dragging out a chair, he dropped into it and stretched his long legs across the black and white tiled floor. It was going to be tough enough without having to worry about unseating an entrenched competitor. He wasn't stupid. No man, unless he'd been cloistered from birth, could be ignorant of what went on between the sexes. Academically, Clem was as well-informed as the next man. He simply lacked experience. Hands-on experience, so to speak.

"Good?" Martha had finally managed to get the coffee maker in operation, and now she prowled around the kitchen, looking everywhere but at him. "I'll be twenty-nine years old next Thursday. At that age, most women have formed some sort of an attachment, as you call it."

Clem controlled the urge to leap into the opening and offer himself in any capacity whatsoever, just so long as it was permanent. In a determinedly casual manner, he mentioned the fact that he had an excellent position with Beauchamp Forbes International. "It, um—I mean, I have this

apartment—but I could easily afford a house if you'd—''
The moment he saw the look on her face, he began working on a graceful method of extracting a size-twelve shoe
from his mouth.

There were no graceful methods. ''I didn't mean that. I
mean, I *did* mean it, but not the way it sounded. I mean, it's
true—that is, I do have— Oh, hell, could we talk about
something else?''

Turning away, Martha snatched the coffeepot from under the filter basket. The last few drops sizzled on the
warming element as she filled their cups. ''I'll be looking for
an apartment, too—that is, unless I can get into a nursing
school right away, but I think it's already too late this year,
so I thought I'd get a temporary job and find a cheap place
to stay somewhere close by, and—do you want cream or
not?''

Clement preferred his coffee black. Nevertheless, he accepted both cream and sugar, and stirred vigorously.

''So... An apartment, huh?''

She nodded, seemingly distracted by the pattern of
blackberries and blossoms on her cup. A soft flush of color
came and went on her face, and Clement stared, entranced,
as her freckles disappeared and reappeared. ''It's the job
that has me worried.'' She laughed, but it sounded forced.
''Know anybody who needs a good farmhand? I'm pretty
good on a tractor, as long as it's not too modern. Ours were
mostly held together with rust and baling wire.''

He tried to imagine her on a tractor and failed. The truth
was, he wasn't precisely sure what a tractor looked like,
other than that it had two big wheels and two little ones.

He could picture her in a haystack, all right, her face all
sun-kissed and pink, her hair tumbled over her shoulders as
she held up her arms in invitation. Her full breasts would be
trembling with each breath, the rosy tips casting a shadow

in the slanting sunlight—and her legs! Elegant high-topped shoes with pointed toes, striped stockings rolled just below dimpled knees and a length of rounded white thigh leading the eyes upward, upward...

Clem shifted in his chair as his body reacted forcefully to the image that had come straight out of one of Hattie's books of erotica. The farmer's daughter and the hired hand.

And he knew who he wanted that hired hand to be. He'd have thrown over a lifetime of preparation and all the rewards it had brought him for a single moment kneeling beside the figure in the haystack. The woman with Martha's face—

Not Martha's face! He simply had to regain control of his mind! "Books! That is, have you read any good books lately?" he croaked a little desperately.

She seemed just as relieved to move onto safe, impersonal territory. "If you consider *The Cat in the Hat* and *Three Little Pigs* interesting, then yes."

He'd heard of *Cats*, the Broadway musical, but he hadn't seen it. And the Tennessee Williams novel, *Cat on a Hot Tin Roof*, had made him slightly uncomfortable. As for swine... "Orwell's *Animal Farm* was rather interesting," he said, proud to be able to contribute something.

"But hardly in the same category," she said dryly. "Clement, are you really as dense as you seem to be, or are you playing some elaborate game? If this is your idea of fun—trying to keep me off balance—then let me assure you that I'm not enjoying it. I'm tired and sore, and I've got a lot on my mind, and what's more—"

"Game?"

"Yes, game, dammit!"

"I thought we were conducting a casual conversation."

"A casual *what*?" He looked so genuinely perplexed that Martha was inclined to believe him. He really was that dense—at least as far as women were concerned. "Look," she said more gently, "you don't conduct a conversation the way you'd conduct a—a train. Or an orchestra. It—they just happen. Two people start talking, and bingo! Instant conversation." The look she sent him was compounded of disbelief, irritation and something more elusive. "I don't need games, Clem. And I don't need any man complicating my life at this point. It's already complicated enough—so if you're playing games, just stop it, will you?" She didn't sound cross, only tired.

The trouble with a clean-shaven face, Clement decided, was that a man had nowhere to hide. Nothing to twist or twiddle when the going got rough. "I'm sorry. That is, yes. Certainly."

He wasn't at all sure what she meant by game, but if they were playing one, he didn't intend to lose. In fact, if he played it well, they'd both be winners.

"Is it my being here that bothers you?" Martha asked. "Would you feel more comfortable if I hitched a ride down to Asheville instead of waiting for Hattie? I'd planned to go anyway as soon as I found out she wasn't here. I don't know why I'm still hanging around, except that this place is even harder to get out of than it was to get into."

"No!" he blurted, bracing both arms on the table to lean forward. His glasses sat slightly crooked on his nose, thanks to having been dropped one too many times. "That is, I don't know when she'll be back—she was supposed to have been back four days ago. But I want you to stay. I don't want you to go. Not now—not ever."

Thunder rattled the windowpanes and faded away, leaving the house in stillness. No tick of a clock, no hum of a refrigerator to break the sudden tension that held them both in thrall.

"Ever?" Martha whispered, and from the expression in her eyes, Clem knew he'd frightened her again.

"I don't know how to say it right."

"No, no, it's all right. I know you didn't mean it the way it sounded."

He could feel his molars pressing together, feel his deltoids hardening into nerve-pinching knots. His hands were trembling almost imperceptibly, and when he caught her gaze on them, he tightened them into fists. "I meant it," he said flatly. "I'm just no damned good at—at expressing what I feel."

Martha began shaking her head, and he knew in advance he was going to hear a denial of what was happening. "You don't feel anything, Clem. You can't—we don't even know each other. What happened upstairs was—well, it was an accident. It didn't mean anything." She wouldn't meet his eyes, and he wondered if she were afraid of being caught in a lie.

Because it had meant something! He had never been so moved, so deeply affected by anything in his life, and she hadn't exactly resisted him. He'd felt her heart accelerate, heard the soft whimper in her throat when he'd torn his mouth away, afraid he'd gone too far.

"It just doesn't work that way," she whispered. "Not this fast."

"Then how does it work? How long does it take? Tell me, because I have to know!" The width of the table was between them, and Clem wanted to shove it aside. He wanted to touch her, to take her face in his hands and hold it so that he could study every nuance of expression. He wanted to know what was in her mind; instead he knew only that she wasn't telling him the truth. Not the entire truth, and that knowledge tortured him.

"How do I know? There's no time limit, but it just can't happen this fast. Believe me, that much I do know. I was— there was this man, and we thought—that is, I thought we were going to be married."

The table jerked as Clem's hands tightened on its edge. "You love him."

"I thought I did."

The pain of it was worse than anything he could ever remember experiencing, but he remained calm on the surface. If he frightened her now, she would close up, and he'd never get close to her again. "When did you begin to have doubts?"

Her smile tore him apart. "I think it must have started when I told him that there was no longer any reason to wait, since Jack was planning to remarry and wouldn't be needing me any longer. That's when Virgil told me that while he would always be fond of me, he'd never really considered marriage. At least, not with me. It seems I was soothing and restful and undemanding, and Virgil needed those qualities at that particular time in his career. I was exactly what he wanted for a—" She broke off and took a deep breath, still not quite meeting his eyes. "For a brief affair, but marriage was out of the question. We were incompatible."

Clem shoved back his chair and stood. "That lobotomized bastard! What the bloody hell did he mean, you were not compatible!"

She had to laugh. He looked so outraged, as though he'd been mortally insulted. If anyone had cause to be upset, it was she, and even she hadn't reacted this violently. "Compatible as in similar backgrounds," she explained. "Sit down, Clem, before you have a stroke. I don't see why you're overreacting this way—it's nothing to do with you."

"I am not overreacting! And what do you mean, it's nothing to do with me? The man insulted you, and you say it's nothing to do with me?"

Martha got up and took his hand. "Come on into the living room and relax. You're overcaffeinated. Have you ever considered switching to decaf?"

He let himself be led, but he wasn't about to relax. Not until he got to the bottom of this Virgil business. Come to think of it, he'd always considered Virgil's *Aeneid* a rather fulsome piece of work.

"Sit down. Relax. Tell me about your job, Clem."

"You wouldn't be interested. It's dull. That is, most women—I mean, you don't really want to hear—"

She could have chosen to be insulted. They both knew that she could never pretend to be a match for him intellectually. But he wasn't being condescending, he simply considered himself an uninteresting man. "Talk," she ordered.

He cleared his throat, squinted at a cobweb that connected the ornate chandelier to an unframed abstract and then said in a rush, "Molecular biology, recombinant DNA—um, an exploration of certain mutagenic substances. Cancer research, that is. Now, what do you mean, incompatible? Is the man a cretin? Is he blind as well as ignorant?"

Martha had to smile. He was such a bold and fearless Galahad—or was it Don Quixote? Had he cast her as his Dulcinea? "If you must know, Virgil thought he'd do better to marry a woman with a similar background. He's a lawyer. His father was a judge and they were one of the wealthiest families in Kentucky before the war. Between the states, that is. Whereas I grew up on a small farm in Yadkin County—and I do mean small. We kept a few Holsteins, but we could've bought a whole fleet of milk tankers for what it cost to winter them over, and as for the chickens, don't ever let anyone tell you chickens are cost-effective. Not when they scratch up your neighbor's seedbeds and get out on the highway and cause a three-car pileup. If it weren't for the tobacco allotment, we'd have gone under without a trace."

"I still don't see—"

"Background. Education. I never even finished my first year of college before I had to drop out."

"But you loved him."

She smiled tiredly just as a few drops of rain struck the west windows. "I don't know. I thought I did, at least."

Clement closed his eyes as if they pained him fiercely. After a while, he spoke again, his tone subdued. "Did you and he—that is, were you—"

"Lovers? Yes." She said it gently, but the words seemed to echo in the silence.

It was Clem who finally broke it, his voice low and even. "The man was mentally incapacitated. No rational man could ever have let you go."

Martha fought back an overwhelming urge to cry, and that was rather surprising, for she wasn't a woman who cried easily. She'd wept over leaving the children, but she hadn't shed a single tear over Virgil. Which must prove something, only she wasn't quite sure what it was.

"Thank you for trying to salvage my self-esteem, Clem, but it's really not necessary. Whatever I felt for Virgil, it's over now. It was over months ago, before Jack's wedding. I was too busy at the time getting the children prepared and the house ready and all to even think about it. When I finally had the time, I discovered that I couldn't drum up much emotion. Unless it was embarrassment for having made such a fool of myself." She smiled, and he saw whimsy and pain and concern in her smile, and it was all he could do to keep from touching her. "So you see, you don't have to worry about me—I've always been the practical sort. Some people just aren't cut out for great passion."

A solid sheet of rain suddenly pummeled the slate roof, cascading over the eaves. Wind blew it against the windows and the side of the house. "My shoes!" Martha yelped, jumping up from the table.

"Shoes?"

"They're still out on the porch where I kicked them off, and now they're getting drenched!"

She was halfway to the front door when he caught her. "Let me go! You'll get wet."

They raced out together, and Clem turned back to switch on the porch light. By that time, Martha was already drenched. "Get inside, I'll find them!" he yelled over the deafening torrent.

"Over there—just past that rocking chair." She tried to shield her face against the blowing rain, but it was no use.

Moments before his glasses blurred into uselessness, Clem saw one pink Nike lying on its side at the edge of the porch. The other one was nowhere in sight. "Go back inside, Martha. There's no point in both of us getting chilled."

He spotted the other shoe and took the steps two at a time, leaping over one of the gargoyles that guarded the house. Grabbing it from under the rhododendron, he ducked under the deluge from a leaky gutter and gained the comparative shelter of the porch, totally blinded, totally exhilarated. He felt as if he'd battled a den full of dragons for his lady love instead of jumping over one cracked and mossy concrete gargoyle to retrieve her shoe.

After emptying the sneakers, Clem pushed Martha inside. By then they were both laughing breathlessly, although neither of them could have said why. "You didn't have to do that," she protested.

He removed his useless glasses and placed them—he hoped—on the hall table. "I was afraid you'd get washed down the ravine."

"All the same, there was no sense in both of us getting soaked." They were huddled together on a small Turkish rug just inside the door, and Clement wished he could see her better.

He reached out a tentative hand and encountered her hip. "But then, I've never been a practical man. It's one of my minor shortcomings." They moved closer together as if seeking warmth. Both were shivering, for the temperature had plummeted from its afternoon high.

"Do you have any m-major ones?"

"You mean you hadn't noticed?"

Clement rocked her gently in his arms, his body beginning to stir with its usual reaction in spite of their soggy condition. With his lips, he brushed her hair from her brow, then traced the path of a raindrop down her cheek with the tip of his tongue.

"No. N-nothing major."

He closed his eyes and prayed for guidance. What did he do now? He was suffering the most exquisite torture man could possibly endure, and if he didn't soon regain control of his body, there was no way she could help from feeling—from knowing...

"Clem?" Her breath was like liquid fire against his cold wet chest.

"Hmm?" he murmured, sounding as if he were strangling.

"You know this isn't very sensible. We've already discovered that both of us are—that is, that neither one of us is..." Her face was moving over the front of his shirt, where the buttons were supposed to be and weren't. When he felt her lips on his naked skin, he groaned in agony. Praise Paracelsus, he was going to explode right here in the foyer!

"Immune," she whimpered desperately.

One of his hands had found its way to her nape, and was toying with the hollow valley there, while a flood of damp silk played over his knuckles. Textures. Never before had he realized the importance of textures. She was velvet and silk, and there was a little mole just at her hairline that matched the one above her lip, which was darker than her freckles. He ached to taste them both.

"It's foolish to get involved," she protested halfheartedly. "We don't know each other—I'll be leaving tomorrow—or the next day. We haven't a single thing in common. You're a brain—I'm a pair of hands. We—we can't even carry on a sensible conversation." She laughed shakily, and he felt it to the soles of his feet.

"That's my fault, not yours. So teach me. I can learn. I've never had any trouble learning anything I wanted to, and I really want to learn... Oh, God, Martha, don't you know what you've done to me?" Her fingertips found the sensitive spot her lips had also discovered, and he groaned as a battery of avid messages went zinging from nipple to brain, to be transmitted to an antenna midway along his anatomy. One that was receiving those messages with embarrassing enthusiasm. "You've got to admit that we're compatible," he gasped. "If we were any more compatible, I'd be sprawled out at your feet, unconscious!"

Clem thought she murmured something in response, but he couldn't be sure, as her voice was muffled against his chest. It occurred to him that she might be suffocating. "Martha? I'm sorry—can you breathe?"

It was possible, he told himself—in fact, it was highly probable—that she might not be as profoundly affected as he was. There could be dozens of reasons that her fingers were kneading his sides, that she was pressing herself against him that way. "Martha?" he whispered again. *Dearest. Darling. Beloved.* Lines of poetry that had never had meaning for him before suddenly illuminated themselves in his mind.

"I can breathe, Clem, that's not the problem. It's too fast—we don't know each other, and I'm not—that is, I don't—well, Virgil was the only one, and I swore I wouldn't make that mistake twice."

"It's *not* a mistake. Please trust me."

Trust him? Only yesterday he'd come at her with an ax in his hand, and now he was demanding her *trust*?

But that had been a mistake, Clem rationalized desperately. And this was different. Surely she knew that. "Believe me, it's right for us," he murmured into her ear. "I could never do anything to hurt you, don't you know that?"

"We're dripping on Hattie's Oriental rug."

"We're probably generating steam."

She laughed shakily, and he felt as if a weight had been removed from his heart. Easing his grip on her, he said, "Um—I'm not sure I can walk, but we could try to make it as far as the living room."

They made it to the hard Victorian sofa, and Clem wondered if he were feverish, hallucinating or merely losing his mind. By the time they were settled in a cozy tangle of arms and legs, the room, the house—the whole bloody universe, in fact—could have disappeared and he wouldn't have noticed.

Martha was forced to lie half on top of him, because the plush sofa was barely wide enough for two. "I can't believe I'm doing this," she said, the words scarcely audible under the drumming rain. "And I thought I was so practical."

"That's all right, I'm impractical enough for both of us."

"That doesn't make a bit of sense."

"I think I was attempting a jest."

"Ho ho."

"Hmm," he murmured deeply as he adjusted her position. Her head settled sweetly into the hollow between his chest and his shoulder, her hair tickling the sensitive underside of his chin. One of his hands rested oh, so lightly on her solar plexus. If he moved it up just a fraction, his thumb would brush the soft underside of her breast.

Closing his eyes, Clem prayed he wouldn't die or otherwise make a fool of himself before the night was over.

"Any minute now, I'm going to get up from here and go wash the coffee things, and then go up to bed," Martha murmured.

The word bed echoed resoundingly in his head, setting up sympathetic vibrations in the most unusual places. Clement swallowed hard and closed his eyes. Martha breathed through her parted lips in one long, expressive sigh.

"Are you cold?" he asked.

She tilted her head, and he wondered if she were smiling, but he was afraid to lift his own head to see. "No, are you?"

"Did you ever hear the term cold feet?"

"Everybody's heard of cold feet. Probably had them at one time or another, too. Are your feet cold, Clement?"

"Not really. If anything, my temperature is elevated, but—uh, what I mean is—" He steeled himself, and the words came out all in a rush. "Martha, I want more than anything in the world to go to bed with you, but I haven't got the least idea—I mean, does a man ask first, or is there some signal? I'm not sure I...um, know how to do this thing gracefully."

And if she said yes? What then? Did he carry her upstairs, or did they go up side by side? God, he'd probably drop her halfway up the stairs—his legs felt like rubber bands! Maybe he was supposed to let her go first and undress. How long should he wait?

At times like this, he almost wished he smoked. Or drank. He needed a crutch. Those blasted books of Hattie's hadn't done anything but get him primed—they weren't the least bit of good as far as procedure and etiquette were concerned.

Martha exhaled in a long, shuddering sigh. She felt her eyes filling, but lacked the will to lift a hand and wipe them dry.

Clement, man and boy merged into one, filled her with an emotion that was almost frightening in its intensity, its sweetness. She didn't know what it was—didn't trust it. Yet she hadn't the will to resist it.

If it had been anyone else, she'd have been gone in a minute. Either that, or he'd have quickly found himself lying on the floor nursing a badly bruised ego. Reason told her that no man as handsome, as brilliant and as successful as C. Cornelius Barto could possibly be all that naive, but reason wasn't everything. Besides, if it were an act, then it was a darned good one.

"How do you usually go about seducing a woman?" When he didn't reply, she leaned on one elbow to study his face. He was paler than normal, but that could be because he was wet and cold. There were spots of color centered high on his angular cheekbones. Fever?

Embarrassment. "I do believe you're nervous," she said wonderingly.

"Paralyzed."

Trusting her instincts, Martha took the lead. She was as crazy as he was—neither of them had any business playing with dynamite this way, but something about him reached out to her and refused to let go. Lord knows it wasn't pity— no man as sexy as Clement Barto needed any woman's pity.

For Hattie's sake—and for her own, because she needed
to be important to someone, just for a little while—and for
his, because he was incredibly special—she would help him.
She couldn't actually credit that he'd never before made love
to a woman—no normal man reached the age of thirty-two
and remained a virgin—but if he had a problem, and if she
could help him with it, then she would. Because as unlikely
as it seemed, she did care for him.

Not even to herself would Martha admit that what she
was feeling for Clem Barto was more powerful than what
she'd felt for Virgil Jones. Steeling herself, she said, "It's
really not all that hard."

"I'm not a complete neophyte, you know," he informed
her, and she breathed a sigh of relief.

Or was it relief? Wasn't there just a tiny twinge of jeal-
ousy for the woman—or women—who had initiated him
into the art of love?

"I have participated in kissing before. On several occasions," he said with modest pride. "But never—um, hori-
zontally."

Martha, her face buried in his throat, closed her eyes and
sighed. If she wasn't already in love, she was well on the
way. Of all the crazy, impossible things to happen to her at
this particular point in her life—just when she'd been on the
verge of getting her future back on track after so long.

"As you know—I mean, I mentioned," she stammered.
"That is, I told you about Virgil. So you know that I'm not
without experience, either." And while her own experience
might be slightly deeper, it was not much broader than his.
And never before had she felt anything like this aching,
longing *need*.

He was watching her, his eyes burning with a dark fire
that made her lick her lips nervously. "That is, you have to
understand that this doesn't mean I'm staying, Clem. No

matter what happens tonight, I still have to leave as soon as I can arrange it. I just want you to understand that."

He was silent for a long time, and Martha was beginning to regret having warned him. Why shouldn't she have this much, she asked herself defensively. What was wrong with spending one glorious night in the arms of a man who was strong and decent, gentle yet oddly courageous? An endearingly innocent man who had only to look at her to set her heart to pounding?

She lifted her head the slightest bit, and her lips brushed against Clem's chin. He took command as if it were the signal he had been waiting for. Turning them so that Martha was lying on the bottom, he half covered her, his weight braced on one arm.

It was a chaste kiss, that first one, because Clem was afraid of frightening her. Afraid of losing control. He was a large man, and he was powerfully aroused, and God only knew what would happen if he lost control.

"Martha, Martha," he murmured against her throat. "What are you thinking?" He needed to know. He hadn't a clue.

She sounded as breathless as he felt. "Of a brooding young man in stiff new jeans and a white T-shirt. His face is all shadowy, and his eyes look so sad, and . . . oh, Clement, sometimes I used to think about him and wonder where he was . . . and who he was with."

His lips brushed hers, pressed hard and long, and he groaned. He was holding her too tightly again, and he eased his hold, murmuring slightly incoherent words of apology as he pressed kisses on her cheeks, her eyelids, her temples.

At last he found her mouth once more, and this time there was nothing at all hesitant in the way he stroked her lips apart. Passion and instinct drove him to explore her in a

manner that left them both melting and breathless, thei
hands trembling and their hips pressing together.

"What are you doing?" she blurted when he began un
fastening her top.

His hands stilled, resting palm down on her breasts. "
want to see you. Is it all right?"

"I don't know what's all right and what isn't, I—Clem
are you sure? You know it will only be tonight?"

It would be forever, but he retained just enough discre
tion not to say so. "You're trembling. Are you fright
ened?" Her face was so close he could see the shards o
color in her irises—copper, gold, bronze. Even as h
watched, her pupils expanded until they all but eclipsed th
gold ring.

"No. Yes—a little. Are you?"

"A little. No, a lot. But I don't want to stop. This is th
most wonderful thing I've ever experienced. I know now
how it feels to ride a comet."

She gathered the lapels of her robe tightly around he
throat and edged away from him as far as his arms woulc
allow. "Clem, listen to me. One of us really needs to b
sensible about this."

"This is the most sensible thing I've ever been involvec
in," he said, knowing somehow that it was the truth.

"I won't argue with you, but you need to think—while
there's still time. A few kisses—well, that's one thing, bu
what you're wanting is something else entirely."

"I know what I want. Believe me, even I know the dif
ference between a kiss and making love. Theoretically, a
least."

"Well . . . I just want you to know that there could b
problems. Have you considered the emotional side of this?"

"Yes," he said gravely. Her elbow was cutting into hi
biceps, which was the least of his discomforts.

"Oh, lordy, why didn't I just let my darned sneakers wash down the mountain? If I'd gone straight to bed, none of this would have happened."

"It would have happened, only maybe not so soon."

"But that's just it, don't you see? We should give it time!"

"You said you were leaving," he countered, although surely she knew that she wouldn't be leaving now. It simply wasn't possible to walk away from something so powerful, so compelling. "So perfect," he murmured aloud.

It didn't even faze her, his out-of-context comment. That was a good sign, wasn't it? They were growing more compatible every moment they were together. An amalgam of minds.

Martha struggled out of his arms and sat on the edge of the sofa, smoothing her wildly tangled hair. "That's right, only I can't leave until I find a ride or a bus that comes within walking distance, or—well, anyway, tomorrow you can tell me all about yourself, and I'll do the same, and then tomorrow night, maybe—"

"Did you know your eyes look almost black in this light? Actually, there are several possible reasons for the expansion of—"

"Clement! Will you just be quiet a minute and listen to what I'm trying to tell you? We're—well, attracted. That is, we're *mildly* attracted to each other, but it's probably just because we're stuck up here together with no one around for comparison, and—"

"Propinquity, you mean."

"I do? Whatever—the thing is, there's no room in your life for a college dropout whose chief claim to fame is her blackberry cobbler, and there's certainly no room in my life for a man who—well, for any man, and I know I probably led you to think that I—well, all right, I want you, too, but it just isn't smart, and—"

Clement stood up. "Don't be afraid," he said gently. "I'm just as nervous as you are, but I promise you, there's nothing to be afraid of. Come to bed now, Martha."

Eight

By the time he reached the second floor, Clem had had second thoughts, third ones, and was working on a fourth set. Oh, he wanted her, all right. He'd never wanted anything more in his life, but what if he couldn't ... What if he *couldn't*? What if he did everything all wrong?

To hell with sublimation, he should have practiced! Most men his age had gone through the experience numerous times, so that when they finally met the one woman in the world who really mattered, they were adept enough not to botch it.

"Martha, maybe it would be better—" Oh, no—even his voice was shaking!

She slid her arm around his waist and led him down the hall to his bedroom. "I'm freezing, aren't you? Is the furnace working?"

"The furnace? Oh—*that* furnace. It doesn't quite make it as far as the second floor. Something about a pump...

Look, Martha, I want you to know that I—that if I—that
is, if we—"

"You shouldn't get chilled," she said gently. "If you
come down with pneumonia again, my Nikes and I will
never forgive ourselves."

The strangled sound he uttered must have sounded
something like fireplace, because she crossed directly to it
when they entered the cluttered bedroom. "Where are your
matches? I'd suggest hot coffee, only I don't think your
nerves could handle it."

"Martha . . ."

"My friends call me Marty."

"Marty. Come here. Please." He was relieved to hear his
voice sounding somewhat stronger. How was it possible to
feel so powerful and at the same time so incredibly weak? It
had to be a malfunction of the adrenal system.

She found the matches in a brass holder, struck one and
touched it to several crumpled papers. They both watched
the flames curl around the pine kindling, exploding splinters until soon there was a roaring blaze licking at the split
oak.

Adjusting the screen, she turned toward him, and Clem
thought he detected a trace of nervousness on her face. Her
eyes would dart upward to meet his, then fall again, lingering in the vicinity of his damp and rumpled collar.

Not knowing what else to do—although he knew what he
wanted to do—he held open his arms, and she walked into
them.

Clem closed his eyes and rested his cheek on the top of her
head. It was like going home, to someone who'd never had
a home. It was shelter on a wild, stormy night. He told
himself he could hold her that way forever, but then a storm
of another sort began to gather.

His arms tightened around her. His breath came in long, shuddering sighs. As for Martha, she seemed to have forgotten to breathe altogether. She was plastered so close to his body that it occurred to him that she probably couldn't have breathed if she'd tried.

With a mumbled apology, Clem stepped back. Neither of them was cold any longer, but they were both decidedly wet, and wet clothing was uncomfortable. Wet chenille was also surprisingly cumbersome, and when he reached out and untied her sash and then laid open the two sides of her robe, Martha didn't protest. Her eyes met his and clung there, and in a sudden attack of nerves, he dropped his hands.

"You were beginning to steam," he explained, and she lifted her hands and unfastened the only remaining button on his shirt.

And then somehow, they were bumping elbows, removing clothes and tossing them carelessly toward the cold radiator. They laughed, and the sound was breathless and overexcited. She looked at him, and found him watching her, and both flushed. She'd worn underpants under her gown, and now she stood before him in only those, her arms crossed over her breasts.

"I never knew how beautiful a woman could be—warm and pink is much better than cold and gray."

"Gray?"

"Marble." He swallowed hard, wondering how the world's finest sculptors could have fallen so far short of the mark. "You know—museums. Aphrodite of Melos and..."

But Martha wasn't thinking about sculpture. All she knew was that Clement was the most beautiful man she had ever beheld, with firelight flickering on his long, smoothly muscled body. He looked every bit as hard as any stone figure possibly could, and she was thankful he wasn't made of cold marble.

Cold! There was nothing cold about the look in his eye as they wandered over her, from her bare toes, curled against the floor, to her hair, which was already drying in a wild tangle. His gaze lingered in the area where her arms shielded her breasts, but he didn't ask her to lower them. Nor did he reach out to her.

And she was positive—well, it was really perfectly obvious—*thrillingly* obvious—that it wasn't because he didn't want to.

Now that she had all but committed herself, Martha was losing her courage. She had never been with any man except Virgil, and even then it had only been three times, because she hadn't been sure it was the right thing to do for so long. And then she'd been disappointed.

Which might have been part of the reason he'd concluded that they weren't compatible.

"Do you—that is, should I have left on my—um . . . ?"

Sensing his embarrassment at having removed all his clothes while she still wore her underpants, Martha forced herself to remove the final barrier. The only light was from the hall and the fireplace, and she prayed he wouldn't see the color that stained her face. Experienced women of twenty-nine did *not* blush. It was merely the radiant heat.

"Oh, my," he whispered reverently, devouring her with his eyes. "Oh, my."

She was inordinantly pleased at his reaction. For the first time in her life, she felt almost beautiful. "Well . . ." she murmured.

"Yes. Well, um . . . oh, my, yes!" Clem said fervently, and she bit her lip, wondering why she had suddenly ceased to be embarrassed.

Because she had. Except for that one swift glance, she had avoided looking—*there*. But she'd looked everywhere else. And everything she saw made her want to hold this man in

er arms, to comfort him and love him and make him be-
ieve in himself so that the next time—with the next
woman...

She shied away from that thought, finding it unexpect-
dly painful.

"Martha, I'm not sure of the protocol, but maybe if we
vere to lie down together—on the bed, that is—then maybe,
am..."

"That sounds like a sensible thing to do," she said calmly,
waiting for him to make the first move. When he didn't, she
did.

The sheets were icy. Gasping, she curled into a fetal knot.
When Clem came in beside her, he wrapped his arms around
he bundle that consisted mostly of knees and elbows. She
was shivering, but he hardly seemed to notice the cold sheets
at all.

"You'll warm up in a minute," he assured her, and she
nodded, tangling her hair against the pillow. "The nerve
endings just under the—"

"Clement. Hush up."

"All right. But I really would like to be closer to you, only
I can't if you won't straighten out."

"If I straighten out, my feet'll turn into chunks of ice."

His hands smoothed a tentative path along her back,
scalding her wherever they touched. "I'll warm you a place,
how's that?"

"Really warm. Hot." She was shivering, but not from the
cold.

He extended both his feet and moved them back and forth
under the covers. "It's warming up already," he assured her,
and she began to unbend, just a bit at first. And then she
extended one leg, sliding her toes along his shin. He was
warm. He was burning up, in fact. Hair on a man's leg felt
strange—exciting. She'd touched the hair on his chest, and

it had caused her stomach to quiver. Feeling his shin and then the slight brush of a hairy thigh moving against her own caused a minor earthquake somewhere in the vicinity of her navel.

"Getting warm?" he rumbled against her temple.

She made some sort of noise—it sounded more like a purr than anything else. It felt like a purr. He was stroking her back, his hands moving from her shoulders, lingering to trace her nape with his thumb, to her hips, his large palm curving over them, squeezing gently.

And back again. The heel of his hand raked over the side of her breast, and she wriggled closer, pressing against him. There was really no point in huddling up in a knot, when he had all this heat to spare...

"If you were to turn onto your back just a bit more," Clem murmured, "and I were to turn more like this—" He demonstrated, moving over her so that his face was mere inches above hers.

"Yes?"

"I believe it might be possible to—um—achieve another..."

"Kiss?" she whispered against his lips. Her arms came up around his neck. As he ravaged her mouth in a hungry kiss that made up in earnestness anything it might lack in expertise, Martha savored the feel of his smooth skin, his thick hair, his ears...

After endless moments, he pulled back, staring at her with dark, glittering eyes. "My God," he said reverently. "It's amazing—the wetter it is, the more incendiary it becomes. Did you know that?"

Teetering between tears and laughter, Martha slid one hand between them, raking her fingers through the crisp hair on his chest until she found what she sought. Her own breasts were aching. She couldn't beg him to touch them, but she could show him.

Clem felt lightning streak through his body. He stiffened. All over. "Did that hurt?" she asked softly.

"Hurt. Hurt?" He groaned. "God, no! What happened?"

Encouraged, she deliberately manipulated his nipples into hardened points. "There's this old song," she whispered. "You must have heard it—something about the head bone being connected to the neck bone, and the neck bone being connected to the shoulder bone..."

"And the—ah, chest bone?" he panted.

"Connected to all sorts of mysterious parts," she teased.

"Synapses," he gasped, and pressing his throbbing pelvis against hers, he left her in no doubt that his connections were all quite intact. "Theoretically," he began, and she shushed him with a soft, damp kiss.

"At a time like this, do you really want to discuss theories?"

"What I want—Marty, I'm afraid I—that is..."

"Darling, I wouldn't be here if I didn't want you." She took his hand and brought it to the vicinity of her breast, leaving him to find his way unaided.

And he did. Unerringly, and with devastating results. A long time later, after he had discovered the joys of touch and taste, sending her closer to the edge than she had ever been before, he rolled away, tossing the covers off and lying there, proudly, primally male.

"Is something wrong?" she asked after watching him—feasting her eyes on his glorious, unashamed masculinity for several moments.

"I'm afraid I might hurt you. Or disappoint you. Marty, I've never felt so helpless in all my life. If I were twenty years old, it would be different."

"For pity's sake, you don't think you're too *old*!"

"Oh, no—hell, no!" He turned to face her then, and without thinking, she lifted the sheet over his flanks. He was damp and overheated, and she didn't want him to catch a chill. "It's just that—well, physiologically, a man of twenty is much more—that is, he doesn't have as much time for doubts to set in."

"You want to back out?"

"Not exactly."

Beside herself with frustration, she tried to be patient, but it wasn't easy. "Then what is it that you *do* want?"

"I want—what I want more than anything else in the world at this moment, is to bury myself inside you and stay there for a week, at least. With options. And to have you want me as much as I want you, and to—"

When she would have interrupted him, he laid his forefinger over her lips. "And to know that I'm capable of pleasing you the way you please me. To know I can make you feel just half—just a *fraction* of what you make me feel."

"But don't you know? Can't you tell? Clem—" She nipped his finger with her teeth, then, taking his hand, she placed it on her heart so that he could feel the storm raging inside her. There was another way she could show him how ready she was for him, but she hadn't the courage. She was only a beginner herself, hardly up to instructing someone else.

"I do know what goes where—that is, in theory, but in actual practice—when it matters so very much—"

"Clem . . ."

"When I'm afraid I won't be able to—"

"Clem!" And when she had his full, if slightly agonized, attention, she said tenderly, "You do know how to kiss me, so kiss me now. Then if you don't want to go any further, we won't. We'll just hold each other and sleep.'' From the sexual flush blooming on his lean cheeks, and from certain other unmistakable signs, Martha knew that he wanted much more than a little cuddling. She only hoped she was capable of guiding them both through this thing, because never in her life had she been entrusted with such a wonderful, delicate mission.

He kissed her. The kiss grew, and Martha wriggled until she was practically lying on top of him. Her hand trailed over his chest, toyed with the cowlick just below his breastbone, and followed the narrow path to his navel. She felt his abdomen spasm and smiled, even as he nibbled on her lower lip. He was learning. It was all a matter of confidence.

Clem savored her mouth until they were forced to break apart for breath. He found her breast again, marveling over the way it fit into his palm. Instinct guided his lips along the most sensitive area of her neck, into the little hollow at the base of her throat and down over the slope of her breast. He took the crest between his lips. His tongue circled once, and he felt her shudder. Remembering how it had felt when she had caressed him, he was emboldened enough to continue his attentions, and after a while he moved to the other breast lest it feel neglected.

His palm opened over her stomach, and one finger edged into her navel. That, too, he'd learned to his amazement, was a source of remarkable sensations. Encouraged by the way she seemed to melt into the mattress, he strayed deeper under the sheet until he encountered the soft nest sheltered between her thighs.

She moaned softly. Shifting, she allowed him access. With a trembling sort of wonder, he discovered the intricate flower of her womanhood. Textbook anatomy was one thing; a warm and eager body was quite another. When he touched her there, she whimpered.

"Did I hurt you?" He drew back his hand, and she caught it in hers and carried it back to her.

"No—oh, no, please!"

Clem's own condition was rapidly becoming critical. His loins ached with an intolerable pressure. All he could think of was the urgent need to throw himself on her and assuage the awful hunger of a lifetime. But he dare not. In his clumsiness, he could hurt her, and nothing was worth that.

And so he continued to caress her, ever so gently, until suddenly she was gasping for breath, and then she was pulling at his shoulders, pleading incoherently, and he could only guess at what she wanted.

"Please—now!"

There was no mistaking where she was urging him. Shaking with his own need, Clem managed to position himself between her thighs. Carefully, he lowered his trembling body to hers, fully expecting everything to work more or less as it did in the diagrams.

It didn't. Nothing went where it was supposed to go, and when he tried surreptitiously to help the situation, his hands tangled with hers. He felt himself bump against her, and even the bumps were so terribly exciting that he thought he might explode. But suddenly, everything slid into place. Nature's ingenious intent became evident, and he heard a long, low groan.

Hers?

His. Hers was the drawn out, shuddering moan.

"Oh, Clement...oh, my goodness, please..."

He hadn't the slightest idea what she was begging for, because his conscious mind had long since shut down. All he knew was this fierce, compelling urge, this driving need to—

"Yes, yes, *yes*!"

And they were racing, harder and harder, higher and higher, all incoherent words and shuddering gasps, clutching, stiffening, crying out, then sighing, eyes shut tightly, bodies drenched in sweat.

Heads reeling, barely conscious, they clung to one another, safe, sated, secure for the moment.

A long while later, Clem became aware of something wriggling beneath him. He lifted his weight, and Martha slid out. "I only wanted to breathe a little," she explained apologetically.

"Of course. I should have thought—um, made arrangements."

But he wouldn't let her go. He couldn't. She had given him the single most exquisite experience in his entire life, and he knew he could never let her go now, no matter what happened. "Even if it never happens again," he murmured deeply.

"Even if— Didn't you—I mean, I thought we both . . ."

His heart swelled with love as he heard her stammering. He knew what she was trying to say, and in a minute, he'd think of the proper way to reassure her. His precious little love was sounding every bit as confused as he once had.

"Thank you, Martha."

"Oh, well, you don't have to thank me—I mean, it was— oh, for pity's sake, Clem, a man doesn't go around thanking a woman for—that."

Propping his head at an angle, he stared at her in open amazement. "Why on earth not? No man could ever have been given a more beautiful gift."

She was growing redder by the moment, her freckles taking on a faintly greenish cast in contrast. "You just don't, that's all," she muttered. And then, "But Clem—I still don't understand. I mean, I know you're shy and all, but—honestly, at your age. *Never*?''

He didn't pretend to misunderstand. Sighing, he turned onto his back and stared at the shadowy ceiling. It wasn' going to be easy. In fact it was going to be downright pain ful. But he could deny her nothing, and she'd asked.

"I was always too young. Well, not always, of course, bu my classmates tended to be years older, especially once I go to the university." *It had been like spending his entire life i a small, windowless room. Not an unpleasant room, be cause there were books. But in isolation, nevertheless.* "Be cause of my age, I was closely supervised. Every minute o my time was programmed, but it was an interesting pro gram—quite stimulating, in fact. On the whole, I enjoyed it immensely."

"Didn't you have any time for recreation?"

"There were concerts, art shows. Plays, of course. I trie out for sports, but I ended up in traction."

"Oh, no!" She held him closer, as if to assuage a boy hood injury. His back had been broken, and he'd spent al most two years in a brace. In his small, pleasant, windowles room.

"At any rate, I graduated from the university at thirtee and went to graduate school immediately. My parent thought it would be best, and I had nothing else in particu lar to do."

Martha found his hand and nestled it against her breasts and there was nothing sexual about the gesture. "But surely there were girls there. And you must have been tall for you age."

He smiled at the memory of the way he'd been. "Th basketball team was interested, but only until they saw m in action. I was completely uncoordinated. My eyes wer already quite bad, and I had trouble walking without tripping over my feet because my head was usually in a book."

"But the girls," she interrupted. "They weren't blind, too, were they?"

He chuckled, and the sound reverberated between them. "I'd have had better luck if they had been. I was a mess, Marty. My clothes were all wrong—far too neat, I'm afraid. Early training. My features, which, as you might have noticed, aren't particularly delicate, were even worse on a six-foot-four, one-hundred-twenty-eight-pound frame."

"But I thought you were beautiful! The portrait, remember? It must've been painted about then."

He caressed her hair, and his finger traced the shell of her ear. "It was a short canvas, and Hattie's always been fond of me. She collects strange people."

"Like me."

"And me, though I'm hers by default."

He was silent so long Martha wondered if he'd fallen asleep. "So there were no girls—no women? Clem, I'm not prying, I just can't believe that no woman has ever discovered how—well, it just doesn't seem possible, that's all."

After a while, he said, "There was this one girl—her name was Georgina. She was beautiful—at least, I thought so at the time. I was—um, I think the proper term is smitten."

"How old were you then?"

"Fifteen, sixteen or thereabouts. My roommates and some of their friends set up sort of a—ah, surprise for me. It was at a party and—oh, hell, Marty, I don't really want to talk about this. It happened a long time ago, and I should have forgotten it by now. Unfortunately, ridicule—sexual ridicule, that is—is a little hard to take when you're that age and awfully unsure of yourself."

"You mean that you and she—"

"I mean that I don't know if we did or not. That was als
the night I was introduced to the joys of vodka. I stuck it ou
for the rest of the term, but I don't think I said more tha
half a dozen words outside the classroom over that entir
period. And I made damned sure I didn't get within rang
of anything female, especially in a social context."

"But eventually," she urged gently, "you graduated an
went on . . . you must have met people. Dated."

"Some. Not as much as you might expect. And maybe
deliberately chose nonthreatening types. I don't know—I d
know I took a hell of a lot of cold showers, and I ran up an
down several hundred flights of stairs."

Suddenly he grinned and rolled her on top of him
"Enough of this talk, woman. You might have noticed tha
I'm a man of few words."

"A man of action, in fact," she pointed out solemnly.

"I try." He made a slight adjustment to their relative po
sitions, and a low groan caught in his throat. "Is it to
soon? That is, could you—I mean, could we possibly . . ."

It wasn't, and she could, and they did. This time, ther
was nothing at all tentative in Clem's technique. A brillian
man, he had always had a creative bent, and having bee
shown the basics, he was more than capable of devising al
sorts of delicious variations that left them both limp an
satiated a long time later.

The rain stopped shortly after midnight. Just as the sk
was beginning to grow light, Martha awoke to find Clem
leaning over her, his head propped on one arm. He wa
gazing down at her with a beatific smile on his face, his eye
dreamy and slightly unfocused.

"Haven't you been asleep at all?" she murmured.

His warm hand slid over her waist and drew her closer
"How could I sleep? Maybe I'll never sleep again. Martha

I want you to know that I'll do everything in my power to make you—"

She laid a hand over his lips. "Please, Clem—don't."

Instantly the dark blue eyes grew more guarded. His hand grew still on her side. "Don't what?"

"Don't say anything. Not just yet."

"But there's so much to say—so much to plan." He scrambled out of bed suddenly and stood beside her, naked and magnificent. He felt for his glasses on the bedside table and jammed them on.

Nine

We need to talk." Martha sat up in bed and pulled the quilt under her chin, and Clem thought that with her red-gold hair tumbling over her shoulders, her face flushed with sleep and her eyes glistening like polished amber, she'd never looked more beautiful.

Nor more desirable. The last thing he wanted to do was talk. He was still on shaky ground when it came to expressing himself with words, but last night he'd discovered a whole new world of expression. And he hadn't even begun to express all he had to say.

"I'll build up the fire first," he said.

"You'd better put on some clothes."

"I'm coming right back to bed as soon as I throw a log on the fire."

"Put on something anyway, or we'll never get any talking done."

He was willing to indulge her. There'd be plenty of time for making love. They had the rest of their lives. Besides, she was right—there were things to be decided. Such as where they would live. His apartment suddenly seemed small, cold and utterly without appeal. "Do you like apple trees?" he asked, dusting the bark off his hands and retrieving his khakis from the floor.

"Apple trees? Clem, hand me my bathrobe, will you? I can't think properly until I've washed my face."

Still smiling—it seemed to be a permanent condition with him ever since he'd awakened with her wrapped around him, her thigh between his legs and her head tucked under his chin—Clem picked up the yellow chenille garment, unconsciously cradling it close to his face. "Then think improperly. I'll help you get started, all right?"

Putting on his pants, he missed the quick look of pain that crossed Martha's face. "Look, I'd better dash down and turn on the furnace. We'll both be starving in a few minutes, especially after—"

His smile widened into a grin that threatened to lapse into laughter. "Now that you mention it . . ."

Martha threw back the quilt and slipped on her robe, and Clem watched every move as if it were the most remarkable event he'd ever witnessed. Personally, he'd discovered that euphoria was its own insulation.

"Five minutes?" she said.

"Make it ten. I'd like a quick shower."

"Then make it twenty. I'll have one when you're through."

"We'll meet back here?"

"We'll meet in the kitchen," she said firmly.

Clem was disappointed, but then, perhaps she had a point. Enthusiasm alone wouldn't make up for a lack of fuel. After a hot shower and a big breakfast, they could take up where they'd left off last night. "Twenty minutes—that's my outer limit," he warned, reaching for her to steal one last kiss, but she slipped out the door before he could touch her.

By the time Martha had snatched a handful of clean clothes from her suitcase, trekked downstairs to the only functioning shower in the three-bathroom house, bathed, dressed and hurried upstairs again, the doubts had already begun to erode her small store of self-confidence. What on earth had she been thinking of? She'd never done anything so—so totally irresponsible in her whole life! What had come over her?

With a haste that resembled panic, she set about straightening the contents of her suitcase. She'd ransacked it so many times by now it would almost have been better to dump it out and start over, but she felt an urgent need to see it packed. And closed. And sitting beside the door, ready to go downstairs.

Better yet, being stowed in the belly of a Greyhound bus bound for Winston-Salem.

"Oh, glory, what have I done?" she muttered to herself as she crammed the damp things she'd worn the day before into a plastic bag and tucked them in one corner. They'd probably be mildewed by the time she unpacked again, and it would serve her right. Her brain had evidently mildewed, too!

She heard the stairs creak and knew that Clem was headed for his shower. She'd have to hurry, or he'd come after her, and she'd already proved how staunch her powers of resistance were. Zilch!

While she crammed things in helter-skelter, she worried over what had happened. Never in her life had she done anything so impulsive. She'd always been the practical one.

Always! She'd never even been seriously tempted to sleep with a man before. Even with Virgil, it had been mostly a case of "it was long past time."

She'd always feared a pregnancy she couldn't afford, as well as emotional entanglements she knew she wasn't equipped to handle.

So what had she done? Gone to bed with a man whose portrait she'd fallen in love with when she was a teenager! Let him make love to her until she couldn't think straight, knowing full well that there wasn't a chance in this world they could have anything more than that.

They were too different. He spoke languages she'd never even heard of—knew about things she couldn't even conceive. What on earth would they have talked about? She could tell him how to stretch five dollars' worth of meat into three meals, how to jump start a forty-year-old tractor and how to stop a toddler's tantrum before it built up a full head of steam. Oh, sure, he'd be fascinated by all that! And then he could tell her about the joys of exploring mutagenic whatchamacallits and—oh, hell, she couldn't even remember the rest of it!

It just wouldn't work. In her heart of hearts, Martha knew it wouldn't be fair to Clem. She'd like to think she'd given him the confidence to live a full life from now on—with someone from his own background. At least she could do that much for him, although she suspected she'd be paying for her generosity for years to come.

Half an hour later, she was listlessly scrambling eggs when Clem came into the kitchen. It didn't help her mood to discover that he looked every bit as uncomfortable as she felt.

Dumping the scrambled eggs into an unwarmed bowl, she plucked the toast—also cold by now—from the toaster and wondered how she was going to manage a dignified escape.

Why hadn't she shipped everything, instead of trying to bring so much of it with her? How the devil was she going to get it all down to Lick Munden's Superette? And even if she got that far, how long would it take her to hitch a ride into Asheville?

"Clem, I need—"

"Martha, I thought we—"

They both spoke at once, and Martha gestured impatiently at a chair. "Breakfast is cold."

"No, I'm late."

"That doesn't make sense."

"That I'm late?"

"No, dammit, that breakfast—that just because—oh, nothing!"

"Thank you for cooking," he said politely. He picked up his fork and put it down again.

"It was the least I could do." She hadn't meant that the way it sounded—as if she were grateful to him for anything—but damned if she was going to try to explain that!

"The post office!" Clem pounced on the change of topic like a drowning man would a life raft. "That is, your emerald . . ."

"There's no point in mailing it when I can just as well deliver it myself. I seriously doubt if Hubert Odwell will be lurking around after all this time." All this time? It seemed like forever, but it had only been a few days. How strange, she mused, nibbling a piece of cold toast, that a person's whole life could change so quickly. She didn't even feel like the same woman who had climbed out of a bread truck to be confronted by a bearded, ax-wielding mountain of a man who had turned her whole life upside down before she knew what was happening.

Martha gave up all pretense of being interested in breakfast. She could no more hide the shadows under her eyes, caused by a lack of sleep, than she could hide her feelings, and she *had* to! Her feelings, at least.

Clem propped his elbows on the table, rested his forehead in his palms for a moment then let his fingers slide through his hair, leaving it looking rumpled and decidedly sexy. "I—uh—seem to have mislaid the ability to organize my thoughts."

"I've never been very sharp before breakfast, either."

"No. Yes. That is—" He finished his coffee and poured a second cup. She was shutting him out. He had to think! All right, if she was shutting him out, then she must be feeling defensive. And if she was feeling defensive, that must mean she was feeling threatened. And if she felt threatened, then she wasn't as unaffected as she'd like him to believe.

The next move was his, Clem told himself. And it had damned well better be a good one, because he might not get a second chance.

But the next move was neither Clem's nor Martha's. The sound of a car grinding up the steep grade had them looking searchingly at one another, then at the door.

"Hattie," Clem muttered. *Not now, dammit. Why couldn't you wait until I'd consolidated my position?*

"He's found me," Martha whispered, shoving her chair back from the table. She hurried out to the foyer, and Clem caught up with her just before she reached the front door.

"Where are you going?"

Eyes blazing with indignation, she told him. "I'm going to tell that nasty little rodent that I'm sick and tired of being harrassed, and that if he doesn't leave me alone this very minute, I'm—"

Taking her by the shoulders, Clem set her firmly aside. "You're going to go upstairs and let me handle this," he said with a tone of quiet authority that would have astonished him had he been aware of it. Not until the words were out had he known what he was going to say, but now that he'd said it, he meant it.

"It's not your battle." Martha wriggled from his grasp and reached for the door. "Clem, I appreciate what you're trying to do, but I'm perfectly capable of looking after myself."

"That's not the point." He removed her hand gently from the knob just as they heard the sound of the car door slamming outside. "Marty, let me do this. Please?"

"I don't even know what you're planning to do," she said a little desperately. "Look, it's not that I relish seeing him again, but if I don't face up to my problems—"

The hoarse sound of a little-used doorbell interrupted, and Clem took advantage of her momentary distraction to open the front door and step outside.

"Odwell?" he challenged, although the man with the alligator shoes and the matching briefcase hardly matched the description Martha had given the storekeeper of the petty confidence man who preyed on gullible amateur rockhounds.

"Barnes—K. Jasper Barnes," the man said. He extended a well-groomed hand, and Clem stared at it in confusion. "You are C. Cornelius Barto, aren't you?"

"Barnes," Clem repeated slowly. He accepted a brief, dry handshake while his brain rapidly processed data. Odwell might have an accomplice, but this man struck him as reasonably honest. Slick, something of a hustler, but basically sound. Certainly not the kind of man who would terrorize women.

On the other hand, when it came to dealing with personnel, Clem knew his limitations. For Martha's sake, he couldn't afford to take any chances. "May I see some identification?"

"Certainly, certainly," the well-dressed young man replied, producing a card case as he spoke. "I'm with Lavorly Laboratories. Danforth said you'd be a good man to bring into the fold. He suggested I contact you." He smiled, and Clem's shoulders settled a notch lower. His fists uncurled. "You're a hard man to locate, Dr. Barto. Your phone's unlisted, your parents' phone is unlisted and this elderly relative of yours that Danforth mentioned—even her number is unlisted."

"Not that it does much good. She always hands it out to anyone who asks," Clem said. He was slightly dazed, having expected to slay a dragon and been confronted with something else entirely.

"Unfortunately, I couldn't reach her to ask," Barnes said with a twitch of thin lips that hinted at a sense of humor. "And your secretary wouldn't give me the time of day. By the way, I believe he's taking a shot at Danforth's position. Can he handle it?"

Ed Malvern? Administrator? "Probably. He's been doing the job since Danforth left."

"If discretion counts, he's a shoo-in."

Clem wasn't particularly interested in Ed Malvern at this point. "You were asking about me at the grocery store in Cat Creek?"

"For all the good it did me. You'd think I was hunting a still or something—do they still have them in these parts?"

"I wouldn't know about that. What, specifically, did you want to see me about?"

"Could we go inside and talk? I have some figures here I'd like to show you, and frankly, I could use a cup of coffee. I've been driving in circles for the past two hours looking for the right turnoff."

Martha had listened only long enough to be certain he wasn't mixed up with Odwell, and that had been long enough for a plan to formulate in her mind. Whoever he was—wherever he was going from here—she was going with him. Sooner or later, he was bound to pass close to a bus station. She didn't know where Lavorly Laboratories was located, but she would take her chances.

By the time she had lugged her large suitcase to the foot of the stairs and gone back for her toilet case, she could hear them coming through the dining room.

"—at least six weeks," Clem was saying.

"I understand. If you've been holed up here that long, then you probably haven't heard about the buyout. B.F.I.'s top management granted themselves close to half a million shares of restricted stock and then put the company up for grabs. The stock's almost doubled in two weeks, and there's no end in sight."

"I don't suppose that will affect my position one way or another," Clem said.

"I wouldn't bet on it. In cases like these—"

"Even so," Clem interrupted as they came into the front hall where Martha stood, purse clutched in her hands, beside her stacked luggage. "I can't give you an answer now. If you'll . . . *Martha*?"

He felt a knife slide into his heart and twist as he recognized her intent, but the pain that had shown on his face was gone in an instant. Long years of habit set the process in motion. Defences clanged into place, barriers were erected, and by the time he spoke again, his voice was quite calm. Emotionless.

"Martha Eberly—Jasper Barnes. Mr. Barnes will be going right through Winston-Salem on his way to the Research Triangle. I'm sure he'll be glad to give you a lift."

Ten

Moonlight lay over the ground like snow. Clem knew he could wait no longer. He'd waited too long as it was. Scared, eager, half sick with nerves, as long as he'd been preparing he'd been able to fool himself that he stood a chance. At first she'd be surprised to see him, but she'd invite him inside, where he would proceed to demonstrate his new savoir faire. He'd learned a hell of a lot, and he'd changed, in every way but one.

Martha was still the most important single element in his life. The love that had taken him unawares those first few days had grown since they'd been apart until it was a physical ache inside him.

Not until he turned the corner of the street where she lived did it occur to him that she might not be alone. His hands gripped the steering wheel. His speed, which had averaged five miles an hour below the speed limit for residential districts, dropped to ten below.

A car turned off a side street, moved up on his bumper and honked.

Clem gripped the steering wheel until his knuckles whitened.

The house was small. If he hadn't already located it and driven past several times in daylight, he never would have found it. Moss green, with putty-colored trim, a wreath on the door and a half porch that sagged on one corner. She deserved better. He hated to see her living in a place like this.

Clem parked on the street behind Martha's eight-year-old compact station wagon. He knew it was hers, just as he knew she was working for a children's clothing shop in Hanes Mall. He also knew, thanks to Virginia Malvern, that management was impressed enough to have offered her a shot at assistant managership at the end of six months if she would agree to stay on.

He was halfway up the walk when he remembered the roses and had to go back for them. Yellow roses. Like the ones on her jars and bottles. By the time he made it back through the scraggly hedge, up the cracked concrete walk and across the sloping wooden porch, he was beginning to sweat. Why the devil had he dressed up like a damn gigolo? He should have stuck to his old gray suit, with the white shirt and black tie. He should've worn his glasses instead of his new contacts, and he should've let his beard grow back. There'd have been time for a short one, at least.

His knock was more vigorous than he'd intended. It rattled the panes on the glass-topped door.

She came to the door wearing something yellow again—not her bathrobe. A sweater—sweatshirt? And a pair of jeans that fit her like a glove. On her feet were a pair of enormous furry yellow slippers, with ears.

Clem cleared his throat, took a deep breath and said quite calmly, "Good evening, Martha." He'd rehearsed in front of the mirror and chosen the more prosaic greeting over, "Martha! Good to see you again!"

She was supposed to say something back, wasn't she? "I—um, I believe we're going to have a heavy frost to-night. Please say something before I fall apart, will you?"

Six-feet-four, one hundred sixty-two pounds, with seven degrees from the best schools in the country, and he was shaking in his cordovans before a tiny slip of a woman with ears on her slippers!

Clem stared for perhaps thirty of the longest seconds known to man, and then he shoved the bouquet of yellow roses at her, scraping his knuckles on the screen door, which neither of them had opened yet.

"Clem?" she whispered, ignoring the roses. "How did you find me?"

He could only manage to parrot his third prepared statement, which was, "Nice place you have here." It was a lousy place. It needed trees and a lot more breathing space; instead it had neighbors ten feet on either side and a moribund hedge.

"How did you—I almost didn't— Come inside. I mean, won't you— Oh, lord, just *get in here*!"

He got. Crushing the rose stems in his fist, he stepped past her into a tiny, cheerful room filled with photos of children and a couple he thought must be her brother and one of his wives, a middle-aged man on a tractor and a woman in an apron, laughing self-consciously as she squinted into the sun. There was a stack of papers and pamphlets on a foot-stool, a partially stuffed rag doll lying on the loveseat and a sewing basket nearby. "I brought you these." He shoved the flowers at her, praying she wouldn't notice how nervous he was.

"They're beautiful, but Clem—what happened to you? You look ...different. How on earth did you find me? I haven't even sent Hattie my address yet. She sounded so strange when I called last week." She got a green vase from the kitchen and arranged the roses, burying her face in them before placing them on the table.

"Virginia Malvern."

"At the jewelry store?"

He nodded. Either his neck had grown in the past three minutes, or his collar had shrunk. He was strangling. "Um, your emerald—that is, she said—"

"That it wasn't an emerald after all. To tell you the truth, I'm almost relieved. I don't think I'm cut out for emeralds."

"Spodumene is nice, too." He didn't know what to say. He'd considered buying her an emerald and substituting it, but a crystal of that size, even badly flawed, would be hard to come by.

"I'm keeping it for a souvenir." She straightened the stack of papers on the stool, and Clem knew very well she was avoiding meeting his eyes.

He refused to let her get away with it. He refused to let her get away, period. "If Hattie sounded strange, it was because she was disappointed not to come back and find us— uh—well, you know."

"She was *what*?"

"Disappointed. That we weren't married." At least he had her full attention now, Clem thought with singular satisfaction. "I think it was part of her annual Doing Some-

thing About Clement routine, only as a rule she's satisfie
to ruin a single evening.''

"To ruin a—"

"I didn't mean it that way," he said hastily.

Martha dropped down onto a cane-bottomed chair an
then bobbed up again to offer him a seat, but Clem didn
want to sit. He wanted to hold her. He wanted to take her i
his arms and never let her go, but he suspected they neede
to talk first. *I know damned well you care for me, becaus
it couldn't have happened between us the way it did if you'
been indifferent. I could actually feel you caring!*

"I can't believe Hattie deliberately went off and—I mear
she knew I was coming—she invited me herself. You mea
she got you up there and then stayed away just so tha
we—" *She knew how I would react—she's never forgotte
how I felt about your portrait. And I thought I'd been s
clever about hiding it.*

Clem nodded, wishing he'd taken the time to write ou
precisely what he wanted to say to her. He needed the righ
words, needed to state his case in a calm and orderly fash
ion, because his new finery—the haircut, the contact ler
ses, the navy-blue briefs instead of the white boxer shor
he'd always worn—they weren't enough. He was going t
have to *tell* her how he felt, and he'd probably strangle o
the words.

"Warm for December, isn't it?" He tugged at his tie.

"The furnace is new. You look—" *Why are we wastin
all this time on words? Why don't you hold me? Don't yo
want me anymore?*

Martha cleared her throat. "You look wonderful, Clem
Your hair…" It was styled, not just whacked off. She knew
little about men's fashions, but she did know a good su
when she saw one, and Clem's was excellent. On him it wa

fantastic. The pale blue shirt and the paisley tie enhanced the intensity of his eyes. "What have you been doing with yourself lately?"

"Thank you. Learning. Preparing to move." *Missing you until I thought I would die from it.*

"To move? You're really leaving B.F.I., then?" *Damn you, why did you come back if you're only going to leave again? I was almost starting to get over you—I was going entire days without crying. Come spring, I'd have been almost as good as new, and now I'll have to start all over again!*

"Yes. Yes, I am."

Clem stood and began to pace, stepping over a stack of books and a bowl of pecans. Three strides took him to the far side of the living room, and he turned and confronted her. Sweat prickled on his clean-shaven upper lip, and he rammed his hands into his pockets to hide their unsteadiness. "Dammit, Marty, I've done all I know how to do! If it isn't enough, then tell me what else needs changing, and I'll change it. I can learn."

She was on her feet in an instant. In another moment, he would have had her where he wanted her—in his arms again. He turned away, and it was the hardest thing he'd ever done in his life. "I have to get this said," he told her. "If I lose my nerve—that is, if I get distracted, I might not be able to—that is, I..."

"Then say it—please." *Say what I've been waiting to hear, what I need to hear more than anything else in the world.*

Her voice seeped into the deepest recesses of his soul, touching, healing, claiming what was already hers—had been hers since the first moment he saw her. "Martha, I—That is, I can drive now. I buy my own clothes." He wrenched loose his fifty-dollar tie and unfastened the top button of his tailor-made shirt. "I bought a car. I took driving lessons. There was an advertisement for dancing lessons, but I don't even know if you like to dance. I'm not sure I'll ever be very good at it, because coordination isn't something that can be taught, but—"

"Clem."

"—I'm willing to try. And there are bridge lessons. Guitar lessons, art lessons, voice lessons and something called ikebana—"

"Clem!"

"I have money. I met with my accountant to arrange to have everything moved, and I have quite a lot of money. I'll give you all you want—for social security and insurance and that sort of thing—no ropes attached."

His back was turned, but he knew precisely when she came to stand behind him. He could feel her with every fiber of his body. "Strings," she said softly.

"Strings?"

"The phrase is, no strings attached, and I can't take your money, Clem." *I'd rather have the strings.* "It's just not done. But thank you."

He turned to face her then, and she was so close—so close... But still he didn't take her in his arms. "But I want you to have it. I want to give you something, don't you understand? I want to give you everything, but I don't know what you want. You left—"

She broke in. "Not because I wanted to. I did it for you."

His eyes went the color of slate. "God, don't do me any more favors like that!"

"Clem, you're a—that is, you didn't seem to know how—how truly wonderful you really are. I thought perhaps after we'd, um—gotten to know one another, you might want to try—that is, you might meet other women and discover what you'd been missing all these years, and I would never want to hold you back." *Don't just stand there, tell me I'm wrong! Tell me you don't want any other woman but me! Tell me you love me, Clem. Please...*

Let me show you, darling. I'll never be able to tell you with words as well as I can show you. Clem opened his arms, and she leaned forward, and they were together. After a month that had nearly torn him apart—a month that had left her thinner, paler, her eyes more shadowed, they were together.

He kissed her lips, her forehead, the velvet mole above her lips, her eyelids. And then he found her lips again, telling her without words how much he'd missed her.

He was intoxicated by the scent of her. By the familiar taste of her, the moist velvet feel of her kisses. Her body against his was so fragile, he felt clumsier than ever, and he took exquisite care when he swept her up in his arms to hold her gently. Without lifting his lips from her, he turned toward the nearest door.

"This is the kitchen," he said blankly sometime later, when he came up for air.

Martha laughed softly. "I know. The bedroom's through there."

He laid her on the bed, and she watched while he removed his clothes. He was a little embarrassed now at the navy-blue briefs. He had a feeling he'd always be the white boxer type at heart, but if he'd thought it would have helped the cause, he'd have worn black tights and a purple cape.

Kneeling beside her on the bed, Clem told himself that he had to do this right—his whole future might depend on it.

Slippers first. And when she was barefooted, he could ea
her jeans down over her hips and slide them off. And then .

Later, he didn't know who removed what. All he kne
was they were wrapped together, bare skin against bare skir
murmured words blunting murmured words as they touche
and kissed and explored.

She was so beautiful—he'd forgotten how beautiful sl
was. Her small, full breasts peaked against his palms, ar
he thought he would die of pleasure. When her lips and the
her teeth brushed against his nipples, he closed his eyes
exquisite pain.

He suckled her, loving the way she gasped, the way h
body stiffened. Loving the way each small sound she mad
registered in the depths of his body.

He was so full he thought he would explode, but he didn
want it to end. "Forever," he said hoarsely, "or as long
I can manage."

She seemed to understand, because the hand that ha
been caressing its way down his flat belly began to edge u
ward again. If she'd touched him there, it would've been a
over. "Or again and again?" she whispered, and he though
that was the best idea of all.

Burying his face against her throat, he whispered word
he had not yet been able to say to her face. He worshiped he
breasts, paying homage to each one in turn before strokir
the satin skin above her waist with tiny wet kisses. *I lo*
you, Martha Eberly. I've always loved you, and I alway
will.

When he could stand it no longer, he rose above he
trembling in his need. "Again and again?" he asked, h
voice barely audible over the harsh sound of his breathin
"Promise?"

Her arms came around him, and she drew him to her, cradling him in her thighs. "Again and again, for as long as you want me, I promise," she whispered.

It was over too quickly, as he'd known it would be, but the shattering intensity of it left them both stunned for a long time. They clung tightly, beyond speech, almost beyond thought.

Gradually, Clem became aware of a coolness on his damp body, and he got up and found a blanket. Covering them both, he gathered her in his arms.

"There are nursing schools in Durham, you know."

"Clem, you may as well know this about me from the first."

"I'd hardly call this the first," he said with a slow, satisfied smile.

She had to smile at that, too. "No, but you see, the thing is, I don't have a degree, and I'm probably never going to have one, because it's not all that important to me. I have friends with degrees who can't even find a job, and other friends without them who're doing just fine, and I think I must fall somewhere in the middle, because—"

"I love you, Martha."

She caught her breath. He could see her eyes darken, and he thought he would die of the waiting before she said, "I know you do, darling. I love you, too, but you have to understand that I'm not going to be a bit of help to you in your career."

"My career is coming along just fine."

"I don't speak a single foreign language, and my cooking is strictly country, and I know that women are supposed to want a career for fulfillment and so that they don't really need a man, and I'm afraid I don't. I used to have plans, but after a while the fire just sort of went out for lack of fuel. I'm sorry, but you may as well know the worst. After all these years, I've discovered that an interesting job is enough, because what I really like doing is looking after children and—and people I love, and maybe gardening, and—and—"

He kissed the hollow of her throat, loving the sweet-salt taste of her skin. "You're distracting me," she said breathlessly.

"Good. That's what I intended to do."

"Did you understand what I said, Clement? I'm probably all wrong for you. We're not at all compatible. You're brilliant and I'm strictly utilitarian. You write articles I can't wade through for publications the library had a hard time even locating, and I read recipes and try to figure out how to use a computerized cash register without setting off all sorts of alarms. Even my emerald turned out to be a perfectly ordinary whatchamacallit."

"Your chunk of whatchamacallit is a form of green spodumene called hiddenite, and it's only found in one place in the world."

"Beginner's luck. At least no one's chasing me for it. Who ever heard of an international jewel thief chasing after a chunk of whatchamacallit?"

He chuckled, and after a moment so did she. "Marty—if I'm so brilliant, surely you're practical enough to trust me to know what's right for us." Holding her tightly, he rolled her over until she lay on top of him, her small freckled nose mere inches away from his own. One of them—he never knew which one—closed the distance, and it was a long time later before they could talk again.

"Hattie's going to take credit for this, you know," Clem said, tracing her hairline until he found the small mole he remembered.

"So let her. We'll name out first daughter after her if you don't think it might be asking for trouble."

"Just to be on the safe side, why don't we call our first one Martha. Once we get the hang of it, we might consider risking another Hattie."

As moonlight spilled across the foot of the bed, Clem could sense her smiling in the darkness. His arms tightened around her, and he brushed a kiss against her hair. Daughters. The very thought of sharing a future with this woman filled him with an almost unbearable joy, but to think of having *daughters* with her, too! Children of his own, children to love, to laugh with, to teach how to play—

Martha had found what she'd thought was an emerald, but he'd found the rarest jewel of all, without even searching. And his had turned out to be real.

* * * * *

⚫ SILHOUETTE®

Desire®

ANOTHER BRIDE FOR A BRANIGAN BROTHER!

Branigan's Touch
by Leslie Davis Guccione

Available in October 1989

You've written in asking for more about the Branigan brothers, so we decided to give you Jody's story—from *his* perspective.

Look for Mr. October—*Branigan's Touch*—a *Man of the Month*, coming from Silhouette Desire.

Following #311 *Bittersweet Harvest*, #353 *Still Waters* and #376 *Something in Common*, *Branigan's Touch* still stands on its own. You'll enjoy the warmth and charm of the Branigan clan— and watch the sparks fly when another Branigan man meets his match with an O'Connor woman!

SD523-1

Silhouette Romance®

AWARD OF EXCELLENCE

LONG, TALL TEXANS

Diana Palmer brings you the second Award of Excellence title
SUTTON'S WAY

In Diana Palmer's bestselling Long, Tall Texans trilogy, you had a mesmerizing glimpse of Quinn Sutton—a mean, lean Wyoming wildcat of a man, with a disposition to match.

Now, in September, Quinn's back with a story of his own. Set in the Wyoming wilderness, he learns a few things about women from snowbound beauty Amanda Callaway—and a lot more about love.

He's a Texan at heart . . . who soon has a Wyoming wedding in mind!

The Award of Excellence is given to one specially selected title per month. Spend September discovering *Sutton's Way* #670 . . . only in Silhouette Romance.

 **Silhouette Intimate Moments®**

COMING IN OCTOBER!
A FRESH LOOK FOR
Silhouette Intimate Moments!

Silhouette Intimate Moments has always brought you the perfect combination of love and excitement, and now they're about to get a new cover design that's just as exciting as the stories inside.

Over the years we've brought you stories that combined romance with something a little bit different, like adventure or suspense. We've brought you longtime favorite authors like Nora Roberts and Linda Howard. We've brought you exciting new talents like Patricia Gardner Evans and Marilyn Pappano. Now let us bring you a new cover design guaranteed to catch your eye just as our heroes and heroines catch your heart.

Look for it in October—
Only from Silhouette Intimate Moments!

COMING SOON...

Indulge a Little

Give a Lot

An irresistible opportunity to pamper
yourself with free* gifts and help a
great cause, Big Brothers/Big Sisters
Programs and Services.

*With proofs-of-purchase plus postage and handling.

Watch for it in October!

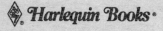 *Harlequin Books*®

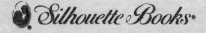 *Silhouette Books*®